TRIPPING THE TALE FANTASTIC

ALSO BY THE EDITOR

Bug: Deaf Identity and Internal Revolution

All Your Parts Intact: Poems

TRIPPING THE TALE FANTASTIC

WEIRD FICTION BY DEAF AND HARD OF HEARING WRITERS

CHRISTOPHER JON HEUER
EDITOR

HANDTYPE PRESS
MINNEAPOLIS, MN

ACKNOWLEDGMENTS

Michael R. Collings's "In the Haunted Darkness" first appeared in *World Horror Convention 2012—Souvenir Book* (March 2012).

Willy Conley's "The Ear" first appeared in Kristen Harmon and Jennifer Nelson's anthology *Deaf American Prose — 1980-2010* (Gallaudet University Press, 2012).

David Langford's "Hearing Aid" first appeared in *SF in Practical Computing* (London, October 1982 in a badly mutilated form; reprinted in full in *Phoenix* magazine, Wantage, August 1983).

Kristen Ringman's story "The Meaning, Not the Words" comes from her book *I Stole You: Stories from the Fae* (Handtype Press, 2017).

DISCLAIMER

COPYRIGHT

Tripping the Tale Fantastic: Weird Fiction by Deaf and Hard of Hearing Writers.

Cover Artwork and Design: Mona Z. Kraculdy
Editor Photograph: Michelle McAuliffe

Handtype Press
PO Box 3941
Minneapolis, MN 55403-0941
E-mail: handtype@gmail.com
Online: handtype.com

Printed in the United States of America.
ISBN: 978-1-941960-08-0
Library of Congress Control Number: 2017942455

A Handtype Press First Edition

CONTENTS

This anthology is dedicated to my son
Jack Christopher Heuer

May giant Martian tripods invade Earth forever
so we can blow them up
with our grenades and rocket launchers

INTRODUCTION
CHRISTOPHER JON HEUER

If you watch the original 1953 version of *War of the Worlds,* you'll find a statement on deafness. Well, not deafness, exactly—there are no deaf characters in the film whatsoever—but on American Sign Language (ASL). Well, actually, no. "American" isn't mentioned, I don't think. But *sign language.* That shows up. This is worth a brief recap; bear with me.

A house-sized meteorite crashes into Earth. It's pulsating and glowing. The people from a nearby town are understandably freaked out. The Pacific Technical Institute sends its best man, the darkly handsome and dashing Dr. Clayton Forester, to investigate. He of course figures out the best way to do this is to leave three hapless locals behind to keep watch on it (a good move, since it's radioactive as well as very hot). Which frees him up to pursue the movie's starlet at the town's square dance.

The three guys left on watch see the mechanical alien tripod "eye" rise up out of the crater and instantly assume they're dealing with Men from Mars. How to communicate? One guy gets the bright idea that they'll use sign language, because hey, *it's universal!*

Of course they were incinerated.

This happened within seconds of their timid, white flag-waving approach. They were the first human beings, in fact, to fall before the Martian Heat Rays. And while this was all completely awesome—the special effects killed for a movie released in 1953—it was also a little bit insulting. Because of course sign language isn't universal. It can vary from state to state, and does vary from country to country. If we're talking planet to planet? Well, I'm no expert, but I'm pretty sure it's safe to assume: *duh.* And if the director, or at the very least the script writer had shared my thinking on this matter, someone might of come up with a less stupid game plan for setting off an interplanetary war.

Now please don't think my argument here is that scene is insulting only because of the "universal" remark. *Initially* that's why, but there's more to it. You see, *absolutely nobody knows or cares* that an ignorant and incorrect assumption was made about the signed languages that millions of deaf and hard of hearing people rely on worldwide.

And that, Dear Reader, is the proverbial photon torpedo that blows up my Death Star.

Why doesn't anyone know or care? Is it because we're a minority? So? Black people are a minority. Is "blackface" still a thing in Hollywood? Maybe it's true the movie industry is still shoving as many white actors as it can possibly find into roles that should be going to people of color (the Ancient One in *Dr. Strange,* etc.), but at least nobody is rubbing black shoe polish (or red or yellow) all over some white guy anymore before plunking him in front of a camera. Then again you never know. Donald Trump is our President now, and Steve Bannon is running the world. We might be back there in a few years.

That is to say, unless we do something about it. We as deaf and hard of hearing people. If we don't write our own stuff, if we don't represent ourselves accurately, if we don't express our own dreams, if we don't step up to take our rightful place in genres outside of "disability fiction," then what happened in 1953 is going to keep happening in 2017 and beyond. *Absolutely nobody is going to care.* And because nobody cares, nobody will get it right. Maybe that isn't entirely true—there's a deaf character in S. M. Stirling's *Dies the Fire* series. I'm sure there's a smattering of deaf characters elsewhere in science fiction and horror and fantasy.

But what are the odds these characters were created by hearing authors? I'd say pretty high, because how many deaf authors are out there? And so where is that going to lead? Sooner or later, what's going to happen? We're going to be lip reading what passes for alien lips—a different set at each end of twenty alien tentacles, no less—from a thousand yards away through binoculars or something. And that's not even going to be the "science fiction" part of the story. That's going to be what's supposed to pass for the "real" part. Or else we'll suddenly all be too simple-minded to drive a car, or we're all going to be Rob Lowe in Stephen King's *The Stand* (irony: Rob Lowe is *actually* deaf in one ear), a character supposedly completely deaf, possibly born deaf—I'm not sure—who runs around putting his hands over his ears and then his mouth every time he meets someone new, to indicate he's deaf and can't talk. Even though once he gets sucked into Mother Abigail's dreams he ends up speaking perfectly. I'm not saying this is a bad movie or a bad book. I'm saying that if you've been deaf all your life, you eventually learn to make yourself look *just a little bit cooler* than that.

So let's get some breadth going here. Just a tad more depth. Let's show deaf and hard of hearing people as we really are. OR. Let's have deaf and hard of hearing writers write science fiction or horror or fantasy stories that have nothing whatsoever to do with deafness (or being hard of hearing). Because do we spend 100% of our waking lives writhing in the existential agony of our identities? At least a few of us think about global warming. And porn. Whether or not we can afford that post-8 p.m. cupcake.

Thus this book. Roughly, here were my instructions in the call for submissions: "*Go.*" Stay in the above-listed genres. But do whatever you want. Deaf characters, no deaf characters. Sign language, no sign language. Deafness as topic, Deafness as culture, deafness as disability, deafness not there at all. Whatever. Shake things up. Think Harlan Ellison's *Dangerous Visions.* Give people something to chew on. Have some fun. Push the boundaries. Bring the field along.

The result is the stories you are now about to read. I'll get out of your way in a second. I want to thank the authors first, and our publisher. I hope they're all out there taking a bow, knowing full well how totally ass-kicking this all is, how huge it is. They're the pioneers that got us to other worlds, guided us through the ether of ghostly realms, took us through time. Without them, where would we be? Let me tell you.

We'd be here and now. With absolutely nobody knowing or caring. Not a world I want to be stuck in.

If you disagree, by all means stay.

HEARING AID
DAVID LANGFORD

It was one of those parties where the decor was very expensive and very sparse, and the drinks likewise. Anderson studied his thimbleful of terrifyingly high-class sherry, and had a wistful vision of a large tumbler of Algerian plonk—a large tumbler of practically anything, for that matter. Of course one should not be dwelling on the alcohol famine, one should be making witty conversation: only Anderson found himself cut off from conversation by the probably musical noises coming from speakers in each corner of the room. He'd heard of the "cocktail party effect" whereby you could unerringly pick a single voice from amid twenty-seven others (he'd counted, three times), but for him it never seemed to work. Perhaps it was something you hired people to teach you when you had the necessary style, flair or connections to be invited to parties like this more often than a token once a year.

The host was doing things at an intricate console which seemed wasted on a mere music system. It was so obviously capable of running vast automated factories, with possibly a sideline in tax avoidance. A different and louder sound of probable music drifted over the chattering crowd. Anderson made a face, knocked back his homeopathic dose of sherry, and realized this had been a tactical error since there would be nowhere to put down the glass until another tray of drinks came by—if one ever did. Worse, Nigel had abandoned the console and was moving toward him with the manner of a snake converging on a rabbit.

"Hel-lo, Colin ... what do you think of the music?"

Anderson didn't think anything at all of the music. Music was simply music, a kind of sonic fog which made conversation difficult or even dangerous. Audibility now down to eighteen inches ... speak only along the central lane of the motorway and make lots of hand signals. Music, bloody music.

"Technically interesting," he said cautiously.

Nigel Winter moved a little closer and twinkled at Anderson with the confidence of one whose shirt would never become limp and vaguely humid like that of his audience. "So *tuneful*, isn't it," he said with a smile.

"Oh yes. It makes me want to take all my clothes off and do the rumba," said Anderson without conviction.

"Ah, but seriously, don't you think there's a Mozartian flavor there?"

"Pretty damn Mozartian, yes ..." He knew it was a mistake before he'd finished saying it.

"Caught you there! You weren't *listening*—hear it now? It's what they call stochastic music, random notes ... very experimental. The composer simply conceptualizes his starting figures for the random-number generators. Intellectually it's all tremendously absorbing; but I'm afraid I was pulling your leg a teensy bit about Mozart. You just weren't trying to *listen*, were you?"

Anderson thought fleetingly of his university days at Oxford, when people like Nigel could with a certain legitimacy be divested of their trousers and placed in some convenient river. "Ha ha," he said. "Music's not really my thing," he said. "Why, before I met you I used to think pianissimo was a rude word in Italian."

Nigel pulled the unfair trick of becoming suddenly and offensively serious. "I do think that's a terrible thing to say," he said quietly.

A fume from the sherry—there hadn't been enough to make it fumes in the plural—coiled about Anderson's brain and lovingly urged him to say *Go to hell, you loathsome little person.* "You must remember I'm tone-deaf," he said, falling back on his final line of defense. "Unless the pitch is different enough, I mean really different, I can't tell one note from another."

(He could remember a time when this fact had seemed a rock-solid defense. "Come sir, why do you not appreciate da Vinci's great masterpiece?" "Well, actually, I'm blind." "Oh my God, I didn't know, I'm so sorry, please do forgive me—" Somehow the revelation of tone-deafness never produced quite this reaction. Instead—)

"Oh, that's just an excuse," said Nigel. "I'm sure you really aren't ... I've read how true tone-deafness is *extremely* rare, and most people who say they've got it are simply musically illiterate. You're not *trying*, that's all. You really should make an effort."

"How much effort do I have to put in before I appreciate a team of monkeys playing pianos, or whatever you said this godawful noise is?"

Nigel sniffed. "Really, Colin, one has to master traditional music before one can expect to follow conceptual works which reject its conventions. Now do promise me you'll *try*."

Rather to his horror, Anderson heard himself mumble something that sounded hideously like acquiescence. Then Nigel was gone, off to adjust the noise machine further, and

Anderson was left peering suspiciously at his tiny, empty glass. As a small measure of revenge, and because there was still nowhere to deposit it, he put the glass in his pocket before leaving.

"What brought you to us?" asked the white-coated man, suddenly and treacherously forcing quantities of ice-cold goo into Anderson's left ear.

"I saw the small ad in *The Times*," he said. "Ouch."

"There, it doesn't hurt a bit, does it?" said the man from Computer Audio Services, kneading the stuff with his fingertips until Anderson felt his eardrum was pressing alarmingly against his brain. "Ouch," he agreed.

"Just a moment while it hardens," the man said chattily. "I'm so glad when people aren't ashamed of coming to CAS. After all, the world's so complicated today that busy men like yourself just can't take time out to learn little things like musical appreciation ... That's what I always say," he added with the epigrammatic air of a man who always said it.

"I'm tone-deaf," Anderson said.

"Oh quite. There's no need for excuses with us, Mr Anderson. *We* understand."

"But I *am* tone-deaf."

"Of course, of course ... Now this isn't going to hurt a bit." For the next several seconds Anderson enjoyed the sensation of having his ear cleared of blockages with a rubber suction-plunger. Blockages such as eardrums, he thought. At last the mold was out, and the CAS technician summoned a flunky to carry it away.

"There. It'll be cured, machined, drilled, tapped and ready in fifteen minutes. Now I think you'd decided to try our Analyzer aid ... our cheapest model," he said reproachfully.

"The cheapest model," Anderson said with rather more enthusiasm.

"But I expect that in no time at all you'll want to trade it in for our Scholar, with fifty times the memory storage at less than twice the price. You could be ready to cope with *fifty* composers and not just one—"

"The Analyzer," Anderson said inexorably.

"Well, of course it's your decision. Now which composer dataset would you prefer? With the Analyzer, of course, you can only have one."

Anderson contemplated the bandaged finger which he'd cut on some broken glass in his pocket. He massaged it gently and said, "Mozart."

"Oh, a very good choice, sir. What was the name again?"

Anderson told him again, and wonders of technology were duly set into motion. The result was a transparent ear-mold with the thumbnail-sized bulge of the Analyzer protruding; there was also a discreet invoice which made his credit card seem ready to wilt Dali-fashion as he passed it over.

"The battery is extra, sir. Would you be wanting a battery?"

"On the whole, yes."

"Then if you'll sign *here* ... Thank you so much. I'm sure you'll find your computer aid a real social help, and something which a busy person like you needn't be in the slightest ashamed of using."

"A tone-deaf person like me."

"Of course."

After playing for an afternoon with his new toy Anderson felt himself rather well up on music and Mozart, rather as his first day with a pocket calculator had given him the air of an expert on the theory of numbers. In the evening he paid a call.

"Hello—just thought I'd drop in to say thanks for the party."

"Why, how charmingly old-fashioned of you, Colin. Do come in and have a quick one. I really don't know why I throw these parties; one loses so much glassware. I'll only be a second, now." And Nigel vanished, presumably to manipulate the combination lock on his secret drinks cupboard.

The room's trendy bareness seemed to shout at Anderson now that it was emphasized by the lack of crowd. He wandered to the intricate hi-fi console and allowed himself to be discovered peering at it.

"Oh! Did you want to hear some *music*?"

"I was just thinking I'd probably ... appreciate it more without all those people shouting their heads off."

"Well, well." Nigel looked at him with eyes slightly narrowed, and then turned to the smart brushed-aluminum console. Anderson noted that the drinks provided for single callers weren't any bigger than those at vast parties—but was he imagining it, or did this sherry taste slightly more, as it were, British than last Saturday's offering? He longed to sniff Nigel's glass and compare; but already the sound of what might very well have been music was spilling from each corner of the room.

"Now what d'you think of this delightful tune," said Nigel with a false smile.

Anderson cupped his ear at the nearest speaker with the gesture he'd been practising, and flipped a fingernail at the Analyzer nestling there. The noise was like a small gunshot; he suppressed the resulting wince before it reached the outside world. "Interesting," he said with what he hoped was an air of deep concentration. Nigel watched him, faintly smiling. Then after a moment, a mechanical version of the still small voice of conscience whispered in Anderson's ear, saying: "*Random notes, 87% probability ... random notes, 92% probability ... random notes, 95% probability ...*"

"Oh, this is more of your stochastic music," Anderson murmured. "Now I can listen to it properly I can see it's just random notes. I mean, I can hear it's random."

Nigel's smile became at once more visible and less convincing. "Of course that was rather obvious after our little chat on Saturday," he said and fiddled again with the controls. "Let's have something of the real thing." The speaker noises changed to something quite definitely though indefinably different, and Nigel turned again toward his guest like a restaurant waiter offering a selection of red herrings. "What d'you think of that?"

Anderson consulted the Analyzer, and after a short pause came back with, "Come on, Nigel, pull the other one. It's random again, isn't it? Only this time it's the change in pitch between successive notes that gets randomized over a certain interval, so it sounds that little bit more musical than just random notes."

"Can't fool you," said Nigel, hardly smiling at all. "Anything *you'd* like to hear?"

"I've been listening to a few things by the chap you recommended—Mozart. Not bad."

"My God, I recommended him? I must have been really pissed. Still, there should be something of his in the databank—" He turned back toward the console keyboard.

A minute or two later Anderson was able to say with quiet confidence, "Ah yes, that's the K.169 string quartet, isn't it?" Following an irresistible urge, he breathed gently over his fingernails and polished them on the lapel of his jacket. Half-heatedly his host caused the equipment to play further noises which the Analyzer rapidly identified as the *Serenade in D Major*, adding the useful information that it had been composed in Salzburg. Nigel seemed a little shaken by this onslaught, and was breathing more heavily as he returned to the console.

"*Not recognized*," said the small voice. "*Transition probability analysis suggests Mozart work, 82% probability ...*"

"That's Mozart all right," said Anderson, thinking fast. "But hardly one of his best pieces ... in fact I must admit I don't recognize it at all."

"Er, yes, just an obscure oboe quartet I thought might amuse you. H'mm." A thought appeared to have struck Nigel, and he punched another sequence on the keyboard—savagely, as though squashing small insects.

"*Not recognized. Transition probability analysis suggests not Mozart work, 79% probability ...*"

"You've got the wrong composer, old chap."

"It's so easy to make mistakes with equipment as sophisticated as this," Nigel said viciously. "I'll have to throw you out soon—I'm meeting someone tonight—but first, what d'you think of this one?"

The lights on the hi-fi console flickered alarmingly for nearly a minute; Anderson fantasized that Nigel's expensive gadgetry, like Nigel, was baffled and irritated. Then more musical noises seeped through the room. Anderson cupped his ear attentively, and clicked his fingernail again at what was hidden inside. There was a pause.

"*Not recognized. Transition probability analysis suggests Mozart work, 94% probability.*"

The transition probability jargon was something to do with sequences of notes favored by given composers. In the long run they left their fingerprints all over their work so obviously that even a machine could catch them red-handed.

"Ah, you can't mistake Mozart," Anderson sighed, wondering if he was overdoing it a trifle. "Even in a minor work like this—no, I don't actually recognize it—the towering genius of the man comes across so clearly." He definitely was overdoing it, he decided.

Nigel seemed to have brightened surprisingly. "This really is a *very* sophisticated system, you know. I'm rather proud of it. One thing you can do with it, if you know how, is to have the processor run through a selection of someone's works and cobble up a sort of cheap and nasty imitation—something to do with transition probabilities, it says in the manual. Of course you couldn't expect it to fool anyone who knew anything about music, not for an instant ... But I'll have to say goodbye now. Do come round again whenever you like. It's nice to see you making an effort, musically, but you really will have to try much harder yet. Old chap."

Anderson looked down into his empty glass and thought of thrusting it into his pocket quickly, or perhaps up Nigel's nostril, slowly.

"It's very kind of you," he said with a titanic effort.

The CAS salesman studied him wisely. "Now if you cared to exchange it for the Scholar model we could in fact allow quite a generous trade-in price, Mr Anderson."

"And then I suppose I'd have a wonderful machine that could fail to spot imitations of fifty composers rather than just one?"

"Our clients usually find the Scholar very satisfactory," the other said severely.

"So will I—if it can tell inspired music from cobbled-together computer rubbish, the way this one doesn't."

The salesman sighed. "To handle that would need a full-scale AI, an Artificial Intelligence. CAS isn't in that business ... yet. Now if you come back next year, when we hope to have chased out the last bugs, then perhaps we can sell you our Mark III model—the AudioBrain."

Anderson reflected for a moment, and then leaned forward with what he considered to be an expression of great shrewdness. He'd practiced it in the mirror for use on Nigel. "If you're likely to market it next year, there must be prototypes around the place right now. In fact you must be market-researching the thing already. It wouldn't hurt to let me try one out a little for you."

Licking his lips, the CAS man murmured that it would be, well, rather irregular, but ... Anderson reached for his wallet.

"How am I doing, Nigel?" he asked confidently, back in the bare, expensively-carpeted room.

"Not bad," Nigel muttered. "You must be trying a bit harder than you were—I told you understanding music was mainly a matter of *trying*. How does this sound to you?"

One of Anderson's ears took in the new meaningless noises that were tinkling from all four corners of the pastel room. In his other ear, the AudioBrain prototype whispered to him: "*Sounds like Bach, I should say ... but that's just the TP analysis. As a whole it's hardly an inspired piece, and the long-term melodic structure is absolutely shot to hell. No, it has to be another faked-up computer piece ...*"

"Synthetic Bach," Anderson said casually. "Come on, Nigel, no need to keep on pulling my leg like that."

Nigel looked thoroughly annoyed. Possibly to conceal this and reduce Anderson's satisfaction temporarily, he took the tiny glasses away for replenishment from the hundred-gallon plastic tank of cheapest British sherry which Anderson was now convinced existed somewhere toward the rear of the flat.

Despite having defeated Nigel in umpteen straight sets of hard-fought musical appreciation, Anderson still didn't feel wildly happy. It might have been that he was tiring of the game; it might have been the AI software built into this new hearing aid, which was now saying: "*You should be able to tell this for yourself, dumbo. Only a real musical illiterate could miss spotting that one ... you're not trying, that's all. You're hopeless. You really should make an effort.*"

"But I'm tone-deaf," Anderson said aloud.

"*That's what they all say,*" the AudioBrain retorted. "*Come off it!*"

Thus it was that as Nigel returned, Anderson was addressing the empty air and saying, "Go to hell, you loathsome little person."

It was another of those parties whose expensive minimalism extended to the furniture, the pictures on the walls, and (inevitably) the drinks.

"Hello, Nigel, long time no see," said Anderson.

"Um. How's the culture, then? Still working to better yourself on the musical front?"

"Pardon?"

"I said, are you still slogging away at the musical appreciation?"

"Pardon?—Oh, that. No, I find I can't handle music any more. I'm going deaf—and not just tone-deaf." He pushed back his hair and tapped the thing plugged into his ear.

"Oh, my God, I didn't know, I'm so sorry ..."

Anderson decided once again that he liked the AudioBrain a good deal more with its battery removed.

THE MEANING, NOT THE WORDS

KRISTEN RINGMAN

I stole you from your tent.

I'm not usually so impulsive, but your eyes—one hazel and one green—were so beautiful I couldn't help myself. You never actually saw me, not then. Not while you zipped your tent shut or while you lay down on the top of your sleeping bag because that night was humid. Not until my hands were in yours, my body against your body, pulling you outside with strength I only have in those moments. Strength for taking humans. I am otherwise made of slim bones, pale white skin, and red fur. A fox who is sometimes a girl.

You weren't like any other human I had taken before.

You didn't speak with your mouth; instead you used your hands. Your family, who seemed to have coerced you into their camping trip high up in the White Mountains, didn't sign with you. But I knew of your hand language because of the way you used it with your friends in video chats on your phone when you were able to find a signal. You used every muscle in your face to add layer upon layer of inflection to the movements of your hands. The conversations kept cutting out, so you sometimes punched the side of a tree in frustration. I apologized for you, but I didn't have to—even the trees understood: blood relatives surrounded you, but you were alone.

We steal people like you.

Humans who don't just feel alone—you're isolated. In a group of people, you go unseen like a fae creature, like a spirit. It's easier this way. Not only because your friends and family don't notice your absence at first. You're our kindred and you don't even know it. You ache for the magic only we can give you. The songs of trees and rivers. The lives of animals up close, sometimes right against your skin. Stars reflected in pools like so many shiny fish. A sky filled with bats and the unnoticed wings of the fae, blending in with the background, as we always do.

I stole you because I fell in love with your eyes and the voice you kept in your hands like the glow of a firefly. Words I could understand better than spoken English. Not words—meanings. The way your dark hair always got in your face. The way you moved through the trees without caring what you were stepping on or how loud your steps were. I wore my fox skin during the day and I watched you, listening to the snapping of the branches under your feet as you walked away from your campsite and back, away and back. I felt the tension between you and your kin like a tightrope you walked with your arms out like wings. I don't know how you crossed that line, back and forth, so fluidly, without stumbling. I wasn't sure I could have done it, not like you.

I had to wait until nightfall before I could take you

without anyone else seeing. Lucky for me, your tent faced the dark grove of hemlocks, away from the campfire and the circle of voices you didn't seem to care that you couldn't hear. I shifted under the hemlocks: my red fur became a long mane of tangled russet, my small breasts stayed hard against my skin, my nipples perked up from the chill in the late summer air, my human ears pointed up ever so slightly. The only part of me that stayed exactly the same was the amber in my eyes that matched the color of my fur and hair.

I knew my own beauty. I couldn't take humans so easily if I didn't have it.

You didn't hear me unzip the opening in your tent, nor did you hear me slip inside and take you in my arms. Once we touched, I knew it would be easy. Your skin sang against my skin as if it finally found something it had been looking for desperately.

It's not always that simple, the stealing of humans.

Sometimes they fight the connection. They reach for their gadgets: the material possessions their inner psyche understands it is losing. Instead of reaching for their lives themselves, they covet the things inside them. It becomes hard for them but effortless for me. I don't care about how pretty they are then—their soul is full of greed and plastic. It's not an asset to our realm. It's nothing that would make a good fae. Those are the humans that I take and I find a way of dissolving them. Of turning them into so many grains of sand at the bottom of a pond. Or I let them stay human. I let them go back to those objects they worship, the clothes they drape over themselves like capes, the phones they clutch in their small hands, the paint they smear on their faces. Humans like that—they think they're witches, but they're slaves.

Other times there are people like you: the human I stole from a tent in northern New Hampshire on the eve of the August full moon. You were perfect.

As soon as I released your body by the shore of the pond in the moonlight, you pulled off your clothes and dove into the shining waters. You thought I was a girl.

"Who are you?" you signed.

I understood you, but I couldn't sign back. I could only mime things that made you laugh at me, or stare in wonder at my eerie accurateness, or nod with comprehension of the meaning behind the words. You understood me, too. I loved you more for that.

We spent the night dipping in and out of the gray waters, walking the Moon's path along the shore of the pond, watching the deep green pine trees sweeping themselves back and forth over the stars. I spoke with you of fae things I had never told a human before, all with my hands making shapes, my face learning to move in the subtlest ways. Your hands were on fire with language and stories, telling me of school and home, your friends, your parents, your dog. I loved that your dog was closer to you than your family—that he was your family. But then he was gone, and you would always be broken inside. I heard things from your hands that made my fae heart ache and my skin yearn to shift back into the fox skin—into the mind that wouldn't quake at such emotions, the mind that would sort them out and follow the scent of the nearest food, slinking through the trees like a red shadow.

Your life made me cry. You kissed me.

For the first time in my life, I wasn't prepared. I couldn't do it. I couldn't make you like me. I loved you for who you were already. A human.

But a fox girl and a human?

It would never work.

I could have kept you, but I didn't. I put you back with a quiver in your heart and a dream in your head of a naked girl in a pond. The next day you and your family packed up and left.

I always wonder if I chose wisely. If sending you back to your world was the best possible thing for both of us. I wonder, but I don't let it change me. I remain a fox by sunlight and a girl by moonlight. A wanderer. And now—a lover of languages who uses hands instead of mouths. Taken: hundreds of humans. Loved: almost half of them. Deeply loved: five.

Sometimes I wonder what that means about humans. Sometimes I wonder what that means about me. It's the meaning that's important, not the words used to describe it.

We've got to let the things we love go. I at least know that.

But every eve of the August full moon, I return to that pond and I wait for you.

THE EAR
WILLY CONLEY

Jessie Sweetwind was out on a five-mile run during a cold twilight evening thinking about her deaf students when she almost stepped on an ear. What caught her eye—and helped make that split-second decision to avoid stepping on it—was the wetness and color of flesh.

She continued running, the image frozen in her mind, as she made her way up to the top of a hill that marked the run's halfway point where she would turn around a couple of wooden barrier posts and head back. Should she pass the posts and improvise a new route home or turn around and get a good look at that thing to be sure it wasn't what she thought it was? A half hour of ambient blue light was left before it would become black. There were no lights along the footpath and the moon hadn't risen yet. Around and around the posts Jessie ran doing figure eights.

Eileen should've been with her. She usually accompanied Jessie on these runs to fill her in on various environmental sounds like the babbling brook, a drilling woodpecker, or coupling teenagers. Mainly, Jessie wanted Eileen for security—she was big-boned, taught phys ed, coached field hockey, and there was no one Jessie would rather have along than a woman who knew how to throw a block or a verbal attack should danger come their way. Eileen enjoyed coming along since she could maintain a steady breathing rhythm, signing while running with Jessie—both conversed in ASL without voice. She especially liked how signing added a bit of aerobic activity for the upper body.

Jessie stopped going around the posts and began running in place facing downhill. Usually her body was warmed up by now but she still felt the dull ache of cold in her feet and legs. A month ago while she and Eileen were running side by side, Eileen heard a gunshot and immediately shoved Jessie on the ground not far from where the ear was. Jessie rolled hard down the hill and smacked her head against a tree stump alongside the pathway. Before she realized what Eileen had done, blood streamed down her face turning her world red. Jessie ended up getting ten stitches on her scalp.

She never saw the source of the gunshot so she had to take Eileen's word for it. Jessie didn't like the eerie power hearing people had over deaf people in situations like this; the same kind of power when they lived on both sides of your apartment and heard just about everything you did—grinding your coffee, flushing your toilet, your burps, coughs, and sneezes, all of your private noises—but you couldn't hear what they did. Jessie knew this because her passive-aggressive neighbor would let her know when she ground her coffee rather early in the morning or when she had been up all night with a male visitor. The woman had the ears of a cat.

Down below, Jessie could barely see the speck of flesh in the middle of the blacktop. Lined along the path were bare elms with branches reaching out into the night. "What would Eileen do if she were in my Nikes?" Jessie thought.

Eileen had called earlier.

"SORRY ... HAVE TO BACK OUT TODAY ... GOT A EADACHE, GA," typed Eileen.

As soon as Jessie saw the abbreviation for Go Ahead, she immediately typed back on her TTY, an old Model 28 teletypewriter converted to allow the deaf to communicate with others on the telephone.

"A EADACHE? U MEAN EARACHE, GA?" Sometimes the old clunker hit the wrong letters or missed them entirely making Jessie play guessing games.

"NO, NO ... HEADACHE," said Eileen.

"WHAT AM I GONNA DO WITHOUT MY SECRET SERVICE ESCORT? GA" said Jessie.

"I DON'T THINK THAT'S FUNNY, JESS. GA"

"WAS BEING HALF FUNNY. AM SERIOUS, TAKE A COUPLE TYLENOLS. DON'T FEEL COMFORTABLE RUNNING BY MYSELF TODAY. GA"

"NO CAN DO. MUST REST MY POOR HEAD TODAY (FROWN). COULD USE A BREAK FROM EXERCISING," said Eileen. "WHY NOT WEAR UR HEARING AIDS WHILE RUNNING? GA"

"RUIN THEM WITH SWEAT? NO WAY! GA" said Jessie.

"IT'S WINTER—U WON'T SWEAT THAT MUCH. WHY R U RUNNING THIS AFTERNOON ANYWAY? DAY BEFORE THANKSGIVING—UR THRU WITH TEACHING FOR THE AFTERNOON. TAKE A LOAD OFF. (SMILE!) GA" Eileen frequently added words in parentheses to reflect her facial expression at the moment, since the tone of voice got lost through the TTY. Jessie despised them; it made her feel she had no imagination, but she couldn't tell Eileen that. After all, Eileen showed a lot of effort by purchasing her own TTY and keeping up with issues and trends in the deaf world.

"THE FACT I'M RUNNING WILL TAKE A LOAD OFF,"

said Jessie. She showed her rear end to the TTY. "WELL, UR LOSS ... XXX ... I MEAN, UR GAIN. CAN'T LOSE POUNDS STAYING HOME. GA"

"DON'T U WORRY—I'M NOT A CALORIE COUNTER. (SMIRK!) GA"

"HA! U THINK I DO THAT? GO BACK TO UR CHIPS, SALSA AND SEINFELD. GA OR SK?" Jessie stuck her tongue out at the TTY and whacked the side of it.

Signing off, Eileen typed, "CRUNCH CRUNCH CRUNCH MMMMMM YUMMY YUM, GA TO SK."

Jessie repeatedly hit the signing-off symbols hard, the "S" and "K" keys, as if she were poking someone's eyes out. She hung up and yelled, "Fat bitch!" to the TTY printout. "The third time you've canceled out on me this month." She'd love to know how clearly her neighbor's ears understood her deaf speech.

Almost near the ear on the path, Jessie went into a jog. She had decided to run today anyway to compensate for the upcoming Thanksgiving dinner. When family and friends asked why she ran every day, she said it was to meditate, but the real reason was her obsession with staying thin.

Slowing down, Jessie glanced again at the fleshy object and picked up speed. When she got to the wooded area past the town home community, she saw a Seven-Eleven paper sack blown against a bush. She thought of the film *Blue Velvet* that she recently quizzed her Lit and Film students on. Early in the film was a scene where the main character, a young, wholesome amateur detective, discovered a severed ear in a vacant lot. He found a paper bag and with a stick lifted the ear into it and took it to the police station, thereby linking the ear to a dark underworld.

Jessie couldn't believe such a parallel was happening right now. She stopped, resting her hands on her knees, and breathed hard. What if this flesh thing really was evidence to a crime scene? It wouldn't be right to just leave it, unsolved.

She grabbed the Seven-Eleven bag and ran uphill to where the hunk of flesh was laid. Or was it flung there? Cut out from a human being on the spot? A shiver ran up and down her arms. The ear was still attached to the surrounding skin that an ear is typically attached to.

Jessie took a closer look and sniffed. She couldn't smell anything rotten; it sort of smelled like raw chicken. The skin was obviously from a white person. Whatever happened must've happened very recently. On closer inspection she wasn't sure this was an ear. It had the shell-like swirl of an ear but it didn't have a lobe or a curved outer portion; they were snipped off probably with a pair of scissors. Two other disorienting items—she didn't see any hair above, in, or around the ear-like object. She couldn't see an opening where there should have been an ear canal—it was getting too dark to tell.

Jessie had the awful feeling that someone criminal was watching her discover his handiwork. She immediately stood up and scanned the area. No one. She looked around for a stick and found a yellow pencil alongside the path. With the pencil's point, she lifted the flesh into the bag. This felt just like the *Blue Velvet* scene, reinforcing a point she made every semester in film class that life sometimes imitated art and vice versa. She surveyed the area once more to be sure no one was looking and rolled down the top of the bag.

Feeling that she had evidence to a horrendous crime, she ran hard in the enveloping darkness switching hands with the bag every quarter mile or so. A conscious effort was made not to wipe sweat off her brow with her free hand.

Getting close to Columbia's town center she passed a brightly-lit lakefront restaurant with people eating steaks and barbecue ribs at the window seats. She imagined the horror in their expressions if the ear soaked through and dropped out of the bag. She smiled.

When Jessie got to her apartment, she put the paper sack outside on top of her woodpile on the back patio. She locked the sliding glass patio doors, closed the blinds, and went to the bathroom to draw a hot bath. Along the tub's edge, she lit some votive candles and piñon incense.

For a half hour she planned her next move while vigorously scrubbing her hands and fingernails. If she called the police, they would probably grill her for why she had this piece of ear, especially considering that she was deaf. Why a deaf person of all people to pick this thing up way out in the woods two and half miles away, they would wonder. Then after questioning that, they would size up her body, poke around in the bedroom, look through her bras and panties, open up the medicine cabinet, check out her diaphragm case and sniff it, squeeze the tube of Ortho creme as if it had some connection with finding the ear. The Rodney King beating and the furor over Mark Fuhrman spoiled her faith in cops.

She held off on the police. Couldn't call her parents—on vacation touring England somewhere. Her sister—already left for Connecticut to visit her in-laws. Didn't want to alarm everyone up there. Her deaf cousin Rachel in New York City, actually her best friend since they were the same age—no one answered except the TTY answering machine. A short message was left wishing Rachel a happy Thanksgiving and to give her a call ASAP. Next, Eileen—a problem. She tended to screen her TTY calls. What's more, she had a roommate and Jessie didn't trust conveying sensitive information to a machine that displayed words for all eyes to see.

The only thing left to do was call her friend Troy but that would mean having to use the telephone relay service. Relay agents weren't to be trusted. They acted as a third party that relayed TTY calls to hearing people by voice and converted voice calls into TTY for the deaf. One of them could pick up on her intelligence about the ear and break the code of confidentiality by informing the police.

Jessie was going to leave Columbia soon anyway for Philadelphia where she would dutifully spend Thanksgiving Day with Troy's family. This was not something to look forward to since Troy and his family were hearing. She would have to go through the whole tedious routine of lipreading a bunch of numb lips at the dinner table and putting up with Troy's lackluster signing skills. He had known Jessie for three years and still couldn't sign to save his butt. They were on-and-off again lovers which made her suspect his hesitancy to fully commit to learning ASL. At least Troy would be someone to confide in. Maybe he would have a good idea of how to deal with the police, having worked as a security guard for a software company to support himself through law school.

She called him to say she was on her way. The relay agent must have been tone deaf and illiterate for she kept typing "Roy" and "Tessie," and misspelling simple words. When Jessie hung up she gave an "up-yours" gesture at the telephone, partly pissed at the agent and partly to avoid the blame for stupidly accepting a Thanksgiving invite six months ago. She lifted the receiver and banged it back into its cradle for good measure.

Before she left, she brought the paper bag inside. She wiped the bathtub dry and shook the ear out into it. She looked at it up close with her eyebrow tweezers, taking her time turning it over this way and that. It certainly looked like an ear. Underneath the skin were yellow fat globules and dark red muscles that once covered someone's skull. The whole flesh piece was about the size and shape of a kid's baseball glove. The area where a canal was supposed to be bothered her. Perhaps it was a birth defect.

More and more Jessie felt that the thing in her tub was a crucial piece of forensic evidence that police must be scrambling all over for nationwide. If she handled this right, she could see herself in national newspapers positively portrayed as a model citizen (and a deaf one at that) who broke wide open a major crime. That would knock down all those stereotypes hearing people had of the deaf always needing guidance and salvation. Her neighbor would finally see her as an equal and lay the hell off her.

Jessie dropped the ear into the bag and set it inside an opening in her woodpile. The cold would prevent it from rotting.

The overnight stay in Philadelphia was blessedly brief. The lips at the table were as numb and dumb as ever. Troy was the same but the turkey was quite good. By three in the morning Jessie was back home in her own bed. She kept waking up thinking the police had entered her bedroom. After a trip to the bathroom, she went to the patio door and parted the blinds. The bag was still sitting in the woodpile opening. Something startling about that ... the whole experience felt like an illusion while driving to and from Philly and yet seeing the crumpled sack again turned it back into a reality.

Back in bed she recalled Troy coming into his family's guest room earlier that night. He tried to slip into bed with her just when they were finally alone yet all she wanted was to burst out her secret finding.

"No, I'm not sleeping with you in your parents' house. You're crazy!" said Jessie.

"Oh, c'mon. They won't hear us."

"How am I to know that? What are your parents doing right now?"

"What do you mean?" said Troy. "They're in bed, of course."

"Is your father snoring? Your mother turning a page in a novel? Are they talking to each other? What?" said Jessie.

Troy looked at her with a raised eyebrow.

"Stop rubbing my leg."

"We'll be quiet like mice." Troy made an unintentional gesture of two mice humping. He was trying to sign "making love softly" but ended up pumping one fist on top of the other.

Jessie winced. She didn't want to be up all night arguing about how he was still so incompetent with her language.

"Please sit up," said Jessie. She sat up against the headboard and drew her knees to her chest. "What are they doing?"

"This is the treatment I get after opening my house and family to you and feeding you a delicious meal?" He was massaging her feet and purposely not looking at her for a reply.

She clamped her feet together to get him to remove his hands. He sat up and cocked an ear in the direction of his parents' bedroom.

She looked hard at his left ear. She zoomed in on it so that all she saw was the lobe, the shell-swirl, and the pink skin surrounding the ear canal. The image of the severed ear came to mind and she overlapped it with his to see if it fit.

"They're watching *The Tonight Show*. I hear Leno's voice," said Troy, putting his hand on her shoulder. "Talking about something that—"

"I found an ear."

Troy quickly withdrew his hand. "What?"

"Yesterday. I was running and found an ear on the ground. Brought it home," said Jessie. "I wanted to call the police but I'm afraid of what they'll do with me."

"Where did you find it?"

"Out on the path that goes by the Black community."

"You don't think that a Black person ..."

"It's a white ear," said Jessie. "At least, I think it is. I can't tell if it's really an ear or not. What should I do? The more I wait, the more the police will suspect me." She filled him in on the episode and her fear of cops.

"I thought I told you not to go running in that area anymore," said Troy. "A lot of crime goes on there, you know that. Didn't you learn anything from Eileen protecting you when she heard that gunshot?"

"Protecting? Ha! Sometimes I wonder if she did it for the sport of it," said Eileen. "Nobody was out in those woods."

Troy put his hand up to her head. "How's the scar coming along? Your hair's grown back." He signed "grow" like her hair was a weed.

Jessie got out of bed and started putting her belongings into her overnight bag.

"You're not going home already, are you?" Troy ended his questions by drawing a big question mark in the air, an annoying trait hearing people tended to pick up. Most couldn't grasp the concept that a questioning facial expression alone denoted a question.

"I'm sorry I can't sleep. And I don't want to be up all night staring at your mother's country cross-stitchings on the wall."

"But you'll wake my parents leaving this late."

"Doubt it. They're watching *The Tonight Show*, right?

Right?? Besides, I'll leave like a mouse." She made a bucktoothed expression and wrinkled her nose.

"But what will I tell them in the morning?" said Troy.

"You're a lawyer. Bullshit your way out of it. If you're really stuck, tell them the cranberry and sauerkraut are doing somersaults in my stomach. Tell your father I'm sorry I won't be able to eat his usual wonderful Western omelette tomorrow morning."

"You've got to call the police as soon as you get back. Get it over with."

She kissed him on the cheek and was gone.

Troy's remark about getting it over with kept repeating itself to the point that she gave up trying to sleep. The sky began to show a tinge of light. Twilight, she thought. Most people wouldn't call it that, though. The light looked exactly the same as if it were in the evening.

Not feeling hungry, she opened her fireplace, made a fire, and sat cross-legged in front of it. Every once in a while she looked out the sliding doors at the bag and then at the phone.

"HOWARD COUNTY POLICE, MAY I HELP U? GA" Each letter was typed slowly. Jessie could tell they hardly got TTY calls.

"THIS IS JESSIE SWEETWIND OF COLUMBIA. I FOUND WHAT LOOKS LIKE A SEVERED EAR WHILE OUT RUNNING THIS A.M." Boy, it was easy to lie on the TTY. "THOUGHT IT MAY BE CRIME EVIDENCE. WANTED U TO KNOW ABOUT IT. GA" Suddenly she slapped the side of her big old gray TTY. Too late! She realized she could've run back to where she found the ear and simply dumped it. Directing the police to it over the phone would've avoided any confrontation with them. She kicked the stout leg of her machine. The printout advanced to the next line.

"UR ADDRESS, PLS? GA"

"5340 SILVER BROOK WAY. GA"

"WE'LL DISPATCH SOMEONE TO UR PLACE WITHIN THE HR. GA TO SK"

Jessie replaced the receiver, made a gun handshape, and aimed it at the telephone. BAM! She went to the bathtub to give it a good scouring. She took her running clothes out of the hamper, sprinkled some water over them, and threw them on the floor near her bed.

The fire was getting low so she went outside to the woodpile. Before taking a log out, she took out the paper sack and set it on top of the logs for the cops to see in plain view.

Much to Jessie's surprise, the two police officers who came to the door were tall, lean, imposing women, one being African-American. She wore abstract, tribal-looking earrings that dangled from her free earlobes—the unattached kind. The white officer had on simple pearl studs pierced into her lobes that were attached.

Jessie felt short and fat in her pajamas and bathrobe. She pointed to the bag outside and opened the sliding doors to let the women through.

The policewomen looked at Jessie sitting by the fire and said something to each other that she couldn't pick up from lipreading. They were probably already suspicious that she hadn't said a word and wasn't staying outside to explain the entire situation to them. If for some quirky reason they decided to arrest her, Jessie thought that the first thing she would go for would be the dangling earrings. Create a distraction by ripping them off the ear lobes and making a dash out the sliding doors.

They looked into the bag and dumped the ear onto the concrete. How odd that the ear bounced a few times before landing faced down. Heads or tails? Jessie tried hard to suppress a giggle. The white policewoman turned over the ear with a stick and jabbed at it a few times. She held the bag open on the ground and flicked the ear into it with the stick. As she closed it the other officer turned her head sideways and talked to her shoulder. Weird. Why was she talking to her shoulder? When she turned a little, Jessie could see a walkie-talkie mouthpiece fastened there. She turned again with her shoulder hiding her lips.

Jessie held her hands out to the fire and rubbed them together. They still felt cold. Her stomach quivered. What was her neighbor thinking hearing these officers' voices and the sliding door going back and forth?

The African-American policewoman stopped listening and talking to the walkie-talkie and spoke softly, her mouth close to the other officer's ear. Why? They were outside. The door was closed. They knew Jessie was deaf. Both glanced inside toward her.

They opened the bag again. Both looked in and nodded their heads, muttering a few more things to each other while looking through the glass again at Jessie. When the officers approached the sliding door, she wondered how these women would read her her rights. Jessie stood up and opened the door for them to let them in. She stood in the doorway and took a quick look outside to be sure nothing was in the way.

The African-American policewoman came over to her. The tribal earrings swayed and sparkled, catching the light in the living room. They were renditions of oblong African masks. How far she had come, Jessie thought. From the beginnings of man, to slavery, the Civil Rights movement, and now a police officer in her own right. Jessie took her hands out of her bathrobe pockets.

The officer took out a notepad to write something. Her fingers were long and slender. Well-manicured. Jessie held her breath.

"It's probably a piece of pig," the woman wrote. "People sometimes have pig roasts for Thanksgiving. A dog, cat, or raccoon most likely carried it off and dropped it where you found it." They thanked Jessie for the call and waved goodbye.

Jessie Sweetwind sat down in front of the fire and looked at the note again: "piece of pig." The fire spat an ember. She kept rereading the phrase. How strange that the woman's handwriting was so sloppy and unfeminine. She was so pretty and had all that power.

TAKING CARE OF THE CHILDREN
LILAH KATCHER

The village was calm and quiet that night, blanketed with snow that glittered under the street lamps. The matron opened the door to the long dormitory of the orphanage, surveying the rows of beds for any sign of movement. The window cast a rectangle of moonlight over one row. All was still.

She had received the letter last night, the answer to her request for more money for this year's food budget. The house was full, and they barely had enough to last another few weeks. Winter had come early with the first snow in the first week of November. The annual party greeting the holiday season was tomorrow. If she could save funds by cancelling the party, she would, but they couldn't afford to pay the fees for last-minute cancellations. Besides, the party was the time that people came from the town and elsewhere, and at least one or two families would leave with the idea of bringing home a child in time for Thanksgiving or Christmas. At least that had been the case for the last several years; the usual numbers adopted had almost doubled the year before. Last year had been difficult too, almost as bad as this one, but they had managed to scrape by all right in part due to having fewer mouths to feed after the annual party. She supposed they could make it work again this year.

If the children ever wondered why the most difficult guests of the orphanage were among those who got adopted the year before at holiday time, they never asked. But then, the little ones never thought of one another as "difficult," did they?

Closing the door, she walked back down the servants' stairs to the warm kitchen. The cook had finished her cleaning and was putting out the kettle and utensils for breakfast preparation the next morning.

The children would not go hungry this year or any other, if the matron had anything to say about it. Her eyes lingered on the large kettle that could be used to cook oatmeal or stew for one hundred souls. Last year she had come up with enough meat to stretch through December. The children had eaten happily enough, though the cook, gaunt and thin as she was, wouldn't touch the food herself.

They would make do again.

"Good night, Ma'am," came a soft voice.

The matron's gaze found the weary eyes of the cook. She nodded.

The cook's gaze dropped, and she hurried out of the room.

Yes, the matron thought. She and the cook would make do. And there would be beds to fill in the new year. The matron cut herself a slice of bread and allowed herself a thin spread of strawberry jam. She then cleaned the long, sharp blade, transfixed for a moment as she watched the water sweep bits of red off the knife and down the drain. She ran a drying cloth down the blade and held the point of the knife to the slot in the knife holder.

A faint shimmer on the blade caught her attention. She paused. From that angle, in the bright moonlight, she saw in the blade a hazy reflection of children, still unmoving in the sleep of the dead. She slid the blade into its holder, plunging the image into darkness.

Her lips curled in a grim smile. With a final glance around the kitchen, she nodded to herself and left to go to her room.

THE TALE OF TWO PRODIGIES

JACOB WARING

The Buckland brothers were world-renowned prodigies, famed for their various scientific studies and discoveries. Yet they were better known for their vicious rivalry. Tom was always trailing behind his older brother Jerry, always being outdone and outsmarted.

For example, there was the time that Tom invented a device that allowed very limited time travel. He was able to send a mouse back in time by ten seconds. Yet his brother improved the device, sent a freshly deceased mouse back to the Jurassic period, and discovered the fossilized remains immediately after.

Then there was the time Tom painstakingly discovered a miracle vaccine for HIV. Jerry did one better and discovered a cure for AIDS that eradicated the disease, thus making his brother's vaccine moot and irrelevant.

Tom devised a scientific theory that would negate the fundamental properties of gravity. Jerry, being Jerry, ameliorated that theory, invented gravitational shielding shoes, and soon after mankind could float on the air. Tom wasn't upset that it took so much hard work to overturn what was once an unchallenged aspect of Einsteinian physics. He was upset that his brother now had a multi-billion-dollar contract with the top footwear company in America. Anything Tom could do; his brother could do better.

Tom decided enough was enough. He was sick of his brother getting all the women, accolades, and guest appearances on every hit show. It wasn't fair that Jerry had won every science category for the Nobel Peace prize. No, he knew that without him, his brother's success would never have come to fruition.

Tom would do what no one had yet done: bring back a dinosaur. He couldn't use time traveling as a method to secure a prehistoric specimen. Tom wasn't bothered by the ethical dilemma such an act could potentially present. Rather, he feared it could cause a ripple through time that would result in him fading from existence.

No, he would genetically change a chicken embryo into its prehistoric form. What was the worst that could happen?

Tom gave his brother a red herring by telling him he was focusing on improving the cloning process that was used on Dolly the Sheep. The distraction worked, as shortly afterwards, Jerry announced to the world that he was in the process of creating a device that could clone specific organs.

Weeks—months—passed as Tom grew frustrated with his failed attempts of pinpointing the specific genes that would enable the entire embryo to revert from millions of years of evolution. Finally, after a year, a breakthrough! He made progress by silencing the proteins that went into developing the embryo's beak.

The embryos showed short, round snouts rather than fused beaks. Tom had succeeded in successfully spitting into the eyes of 40-50 million years of evolution! Next he focused on the limbs and eventually succeeded in producing velociraptor-shaped legs.

After a few years of development, the embryos went from looking like chicks to looking like miniature dinosaurs. There was only one problem: none of the eggs were hatching.

While waiting to see if his most recent batch of eggs would have more success, his phone buzzed with a news alert. He clicked on the notification prompt, read the breaking news, and screamed. Jerry was able to clone human organs that were compatible with all those who needed transplants.

Behind him, one of the eggs hatched. He turned to see a miniaturized feathered dinosaur. Its face was yellow. Its entire body was covered with tan feathers with the exception of its wings which were a hue of blue. Tom recognized the newly hatched creature to be an Archaeopteryx.

This was it! The moment he needed to finally come out on top of his brother. To finally be the one in the spotlight. Where the ladies would fall all over him, where he could finally appear on *Star Trek: Galaxies Beyond* and maybe even open a dinosaur safari!

The possibilities were endless. Of course, Tom simply had to rub it into his brother's face first. He called his brother, mumbling something about wanting to congratulate Jerry on his recent achievement. Could they meet at his lab?

Tom arrived at his brother's laboratory an hour later with wine in one hand and the steel box that held his little feathered friend in the other. They drank, laughed, and acted like caring brothers for once.

Jerry inquired tipsily about what was in the box. Tom explained, amping up the dramatics, how he defied evolution, and instigated the second coming of the dinosaurs. He kicked open the box, and out came a hen-sized, chubby Archaeopteryx.

Kneeling, Jerry petted the creature as it cooed, noting that it was *cute.*

A vein throbbed on Tom's forehead as he seethed. How dare his brother act so cavalier about his creation!

Jerry shrugged, produced a remote, and proceeded to open a door at the other end of the lab that led into an enclosure.

Out stomped a Theropod, a gnarly dinosaur that was slightly bigger than an ostrich. Its long legs and arms swept across the room and it sniffed at the smaller dinosaur. It promptly ate and gulped down the Archaeopteryx.

Tom was stunned into silence. His brother explained that he brought the Beishanlong back from extinction. He suspected what Tom was up to and finished long before Tom's first actual breakthrough. Jerry only proceeded to produce cloned organs as he grew tired of waiting for his brother to catch up.

Enraged, Tom charged at Jerry; he couldn't once again be outdone, outmaneuvered like this! Made a fool by his own brother! He would blame his death on the dinosaur.

Jerry sidestepped and Tom crashed into the enclosure. The door slammed shut. To his horror, Tom heard the growling of Jerry's Beishanlong.

Jerry drank the rest of the wine, serenaded to a deep slumber by the screams of his disemboweled brother.

STARTING FROM SCRATCH

KRIS ASHTON

Peering around to make sure he was unobserved, John Smythwick carried a brown paper bag across the parking lot, got in his car, and shut the door. He tossed the paper bag on the passenger seat and took his mobile phone from his pocket. Blinding sparks reflected off the letters that spelled BRAYSHAW BIO-TECH across the building's front. John flicked the car's sun visor down and tapped through his phone's contact list.

He had entered the name so long ago he couldn't remember what it was—only that it started with a "D." He scrolled down until he found it, Davison Enterprises, and made the call.

The phone at the other end rang once before it was picked up.

"You have something?" said a man's voice.

"Something huge," John said, trying to sound cool and impassive like the stranger he was speaking to. "The fastest fatality I've ever seen. It affects the adrenal glands and red blood cells. The rate of replication—"

"You have seen it in action?" the man said.

"With my own two eyes. More than once."

"Human subjects?"

"Not yet, but it was engineered such that the species shouldn't matter. Trust me, when you see it in action you're going to—"

"When can you deliver?"

John thought quickly. "Six-thirty this evening."

"Very well. Payment will be made on delivery. Do you remember the delivery point?"

"Of course. I've driven past it five days a week for the past two years."

"Call if the plan is compromised."

The stranger hung up in his ear. John put the phone back in his pocket. He took two calming breaths and removed a sandwich from the brown paper bag. His knotted stomach wanted nothing to do with food, but John knew that having low blood sugar could be dangerous.

Fifteen minutes later he returned to the lab, waving his pass at the sensor for the outer door. Three fumigated keeper suits hung from wall hooks. Beside them was a small door that accessed the fumigation chamber. John stepped into a suit, drew it over his shoulders, and zipped it up. He pulled on the hood, which had a clear plastic faceplate, and sealed it around the neck of his jumpsuit. A meshed eyelet below the faceplate allowed air in and out, although it had a flap above it that could quickly create a seal if necessary.

John went to a second door, where he punched in a passcode to gain access. Banks of fluorescent lights washed all but the faintest shadows from the lab. In the center was a long bench upon which sat two microscopes and a range of other equipment. Desks and computer terminals abutted the left and right walls, while at the back wall were rows of clear plastic cages ventilated with a fine mesh that permitted only air. Inside the cages on the left were half a dozen rats and mice that perpetually sniffed the air and twitched their tiny whiskers.

The cages on the right were smeared a deep maroon. If a person were to get close enough, he or she might see tiny black insects crawling through matted hair or springing high to seek escape.

John hated the little bastards. If he never saw another flea in his life, that would be fine with him.

George, the chief scientist on the project, coded his way into the lab a short while later. He closed the door and sat beside John on one of the two high-backed stools attending the bench.

"Missed you at lunch time," he said, his voice slightly muffled by the facemask's thin plastic film.

"I had a personal phone call to make."

"Nothing bad, I hope?"

"Just family stuff. You know, the usual overblown dramas you get with a kid at uni and an ancient mother-in-law."

George laughed. "All too well, I'm afraid. And it's Dad who has to be there to solve all the problems. Usually with his wallet."

"That's about the size of it."

The real size of it was that John had invented his wife, kids, and mother-in-law shortly after taking the job at Brayshaw Biotech. He would be glad to let them vanish into nothingness again—keeping track of their names and the important events in their lives was much trickier than bio-engineering.

"Speaking of size, I think we're ready to try a larger species," George said.

On one of the computer desks was a cage that, except for its dimensions, was identical to those containing the rats. Inside, a white rabbit sat timid and confused, its pink eyes absorbing the nothingness of its plastic prison.

George lifted the cage and put it into an isolation chamber that resembled a large humidicrib, like that used in hospital maternity wards for premature babies. The rabbit scratched at the floor of the cage with its forepaws and made a few feeble hops before accepting its futile situation.

John went to another shelf, this one lined with plastic specimen jars. He picked one that had *Itch v.5* written on it in black marker and put it next to the rabbit cage. Then he sealed the isolation chamber and put his hands into the rubber access gloves that lay limp inside the chamber wall.

"Ready?" George asked.

John nodded and George slid back a hatch in the top of the cage. The rabbit made a skittish jump, as if sensing something sinister afoot. John opened the specimen jar and dropped it in the cage. George slid the hatch into place again and he and John stepped back to watch.

The fleas sprang from the jar, drawn to the intoxicating smell of rabbit blood. The rabbit's nose began to twitch faster and it shook its head as one of the fleas leaped into its ear. Then the rabbit scratched its neck, first with its left leg and then its right.

A moment later the rabbit began to squeal. It hopped up and down in the cage, almost tipping it over. One of the rabbit's eyes went first, bursting like a gooseberry squished between invisible fingers. Blood splattered against the cage and speckled the rabbit's white fur. More blood vomited from its mouth and then the second eye ruptured. The rabbit let out a long shriek and fell on its side, its back legs kicking out and leaving red claw marks on the casing. Its skin stretched and veins became visible beneath its fur.

A savage rigor shook its body and its mouth yawed, the exposed teeth giving it a predatory look. More blood ran from its ears and its anus began to swell, inflating like a fluffy white balloon. It burst with an audible pop, spraying the cage with gore, and the rabbit was all but still, its paws jittering in final death throes.

Fleas sprang about the cage, as if celebrating the murder of an abhorrent dictator.

"Just over two minutes," George said, holding up the stopwatch so John could see its display.

He nodded. "Even quicker than some of the rats. An excellent result."

For the next four hours John worked with George to conduct other tests and compile more data for their report. As the wall clock circled past five p.m., he found himself becoming jumpy and unable to concentrate.

At around quarter to six, George stood up and stretched. "I think I've had enough for one day," he said. "I'm going cross-eyed."

John turned in his seat and tried to look distracted. "I might need to come in a bit late tomorrow, so I think I'll put in another hour or two."

"Okay. Don't fall asleep at the desk—you might break something expensive."

That was George's standard witty remark whenever John worked late. Another thing John wouldn't miss about Brayshaw Biotech.

"Bye, George."

George pressed a button and the door opened to the adjoining change room. After he'd walked through, the door whispered shut again. John listened for the familiar hiss as George fumigated his suit. He watched the clock tick through another minute and heard the faint sound of footsteps and the clicks of the outer door opening and shutting.

Using that final click as his cue, he stood up and went to the rows of blood-spattered cages. He scrutinized each, looking for the liveliest flea colonies. The two most recent rat tests appeared to be the best options; the cases swarmed with minuscule brown-black bodies.

He picked up the cases and studied each carefully to ensure that neither the hatches nor the mesh had been compromised. Then he stacked one upon the other and pressed the button to exit the laboratory.

He put the cages on a bench and stepped into the fumigation chamber. He sealed the door and connected the eyelet in his suit to an airhose that hung down from the wall like an elephant's trunk. When that was done he pressed a button and the chamber filled with white gas. After ninety seconds an exhaust fan activated and sucked the gas back out. Water then sprayed down from above, washing the condensed gas from the suit's shiny surface.

Back in the change room John stripped off his suit and hung it on the hook provided. He also took off his jacket.

He looked at his watch and saw it was a few minutes after six. He doubted he would pass anyone on the way to his car, but there was no sense taking a chance. He put the first cage in the crook of his elbow and balanced the second cage on top of it. He covered both with his jacket. The corners looked a tad suspect, but so long as the cages' gory contents were not on show he figured he'd be okay.

He took a deep breath to slow his heart and clear his mind. As he was about to press the button to exit, the door swished open and he found himself face-to-face with George.

George's eyes darted from John to the bundle in his arm and back to John again. In that second, John saw himself as George must have: mouth open, eyes stunned, and the ridiculous geometric shape of his jacket seconding the guilt written across his face.

He expected George to say something cinematic like, "John ... John, what are you doing with those cages?"

But George only tensed into a crouch, as if to lunge at him. Then he gave the jacket a doubtful look and licked his lips. The outer door hissed shut. George extended his arms. "Give me the cages, John."

"Get out of my way."

George made a grab for the cages and John tucked them in tight to his body, as if they were a pair of footballs. The men eyed each other, grunting as they took part in a delicate yet determined tug-o'-war. George was older than John but his sinewy forearms had an alarming strength and John could feel one of the cages being slowly pried from his grasp.

But then George's sweaty hands slipped off and John stumbled backwards, colliding heavily with the wall. He pushed off and screamed in George's face, "You want to kill us both, you fucking maniac?"

Doubt and fear flashed in George's eyes. Seeing his attention diverted, John launched his knee as hard as he dared, mashing George's testicles. George looked at John with an almost Caesarean expression of betrayal—*et tu, Brutus?*—and fell against the wall with both hands cupping his groin. John waited for him to collapse, but instead he emitted a furious noise and staggered to his full enraged height again, eyes aflame.

He made a grab for the cages, and John thrust one into his hands. George blinked at it, astonished, and John headbutted him.

The chief scientist rocked back, blood already spurting from his nose, and fell full-length onto the hard floor. The lid popped off the cage and George found himself eye to eye with a dead rat. He batted it away and clawed at his face, screaming the scream of a living dead man.

John stooped to pick up his jacket and slapped the outer door's exit button before George could make another rush for him and before the fleas decided to migrate. He needn't have worried about George, however; as the outer door slipped shut again, he saw his former colleague making a lunatic rush for the fumigation chamber.

John draped his jacket over the remaining cage and walked at a quick but sensible pace toward the front door. He mused that he might be able to sell Davison Enterprises some extra information: results on a human test subject. What would that fetch? An extra million at least. Maybe two. He passed no one in the corridor and the parking lot was empty. He got in his car, putting the cage carefully on the passenger's seat, and slammed the door. *I did it,* he thought as he started the engine. *I might actually pull this off.*

Paranoia tormented his mind as he backed the car out. He half expected shouting security guards to explode from the front door and try to chase him down. But when he turned right and joined the flow of traffic, an opiated grin stretched across his face.

"I made it," he said.

When he pulled over at the delivery point he glanced at the car's in-dash clock, which put the time at 6:26. The park bench where he was to make the trade was unoccupied. He didn't know what his contact at Davison Enterprises looked like, but the evening had grown chilly and few souls haunted the park.

He pondered how to best renegotiate the deal. Perhaps he would leave the cage in the car until his contact made some calls and secured the extra cash. John scratched absently at his hand, just below the little finger. Then he felt a sharp sting behind his ear, where his hairline met his neck. He slapped his hand down hard and raked it back until the sting site was under the tip of his index finger. He pinched his finger and thumb together and held them up in the dying light.

The flea lay motionless for a second and then started to move its legs. John closed his fingers again, but the flea jumped away and disappeared, its size providing perfect camouflage.

With a trembling hand John lifted his jacket away from the cage. The lid was still in place and the mesh appeared undamaged. He almost let himself feel relief—to entertain the idea he had been the victim of an almost impossible coincidence—when he saw one corner of the cage had cracked, leaving a gap between the side of the casing and the lid.

Another bite. This time inside his shirt.

Terrified tears prickled his eyes. His chin jittered as he felt another bite on his neck and then one on the back of his head.

First gibbering and then shrieking, he fumbled open the door and spilled out of the car. He got as far as the footpath that encircled the park before his eyes started to pulse and a lightning bolt of pain exploded through his head.

An adrenaline dam burst and sluiced into his veins. His twitching legs dumped him onto the concrete and he tasted blood in his mouth. All his muscles tensed up in unison and his ears seemed to inflate from the inside.

There was a tremendous bang as his left eardrum ruptured. The agony was unspeakable, a barrel from hell's finest reserve. Before John could respond with a scream the right eardrum went as well, filling the canal with blood. John knew he had to be deaf, but a piercing ring tormented him nonetheless.

His chest and abdomen began to tighten, as if his ribs were crushing the organs within. But he knew from his experiments that the converse was true: the organs were expanding with blood. As he lay there paralyzed in a perfect adrenaline panic he saw an image of the rabbit, its bowel engorging with blood until it blasted out of its anus.

John's eyes popped simultaneously, spilling black liquid down his cheeks. Though deaf and blind, he could still see the rabbit and hear its squeal as the flea-venom turned its circulatory system from giver of life to giver of death.

John Smythwick lay in the park, praying for the vessels in his brain to rupture.

Frank Redman walked through the park, his beagle Otis straining at the end of his leash. Usually Otis wanted to visit the trees and check for calling cards, but tonight he seemed desperate to get to the far side of the park. When they rejoined the path, Otis doubled his efforts and nearly tugged Frank's shoulder out of its socket.

"What's your hurry, you crazy mutt?"

The park's photosensitive lamplights flickered into life and illuminated a man stretched out on his side, his hands clenched into claws. The flesh of his ruptured eyeballs hung on his cheeks. Blood from his open mouth had pooled on the footpath while a second, smaller pond had formed below the seat of his pants.

Frank clapped a hand over his mouth and reached into his pocket for a phone that sat charging on the sideboard at home. He looked in vain for another citizen before spotting, on a distant street corner, the reassuring light of a public phone.

Frank started toward it, but the leash pulled taut in his hand. He turned back to see Otis scratching his face.

"Come on, boy, let's go," Frank said.

RUI'S STORY
BOBBY COX & JOANNE YEE

We sat with a freshly poured cup of beer at our glass kitchen table at home. Meifawn was playing with an apple in her hands. After a while, she put it down on the table and looked at me.

"The most amazing thing happened last week," Meifawn said with a wide smile. She reached out to poke my arm. "Rui is starting to pick up more language. We talked about boys on the moon!"

I raised my eyebrows and nodded for her to go on. Meifawn brushed aside some of her long black hair that was blocking her eyes. As she did, the light caught the diamond of her engagement ring. Our engagement ring. Its reflections shimmied on the wall as she spoke with her hands.

"But first, do you remember Rui? The boy who came into the classroom at the beginning of the year with very little language?"

"I remember," I said. "I also remember something about him creating tiny buses on his desk? Was that last week?"

"Yes!" Meifawn exclaimed. "Those tiny buses were so cute!" She frowned and looked down at the table, then shook her head. "Miss Rose, the teacher is taking away their birthright, their language. I don't know if I told you this, but after Rui started to make all kinds of buses in so many different sizes and colors, the teacher interrupted him by brushing aside everything he had created. Pop. They all disappeared. Then she forced him to spell the English word 'BUS' on the chalkboard."

"What? She didn't take the opportunity to help Rui open up?" I said. "Trying to force English down these kids' throats like ..."

"Yeah. She yelled at Rui. He looked so sad, upset, and confused. I don't think she can see very well the creations they make." Meifawn sighed. "It seems so obvious to me the best way to reach Rui is through this visual play."

I shook my head. It weighed heavily on us any time that someone didn't understand how special these children were and pushed them to act and try to be *normal.*

"But last week I was sitting with Rui in the classroom, and we were looking at an old book called *The Little Prince.* I was pointing at the pictures and explaining to Rui what some of them were. Planets, moons, and little boys!"

I smiled at the thought.

Meifawn took a sip from the beer. "Then all of a sudden, Rui-created a little blue boy sitting on the moon! Right in between his hands! It was so clear. And so well-done ..." Meifawn trailed off, smiled, and started to brush off the condensation on the side of the beer.

I asked, "Did he keep going? Was that it?"

"That was all," she said. "Reading time was over, and we had to move on to other things."

I frowned. "Wow, just like that? Nobody saw? Not even Miss Rose?"

"Yeah," Meifawn said. "Just like that. Nobody saw. They never do."

"Never?"

"Never. Even though she's a trained teacher, Miss Rose just doesn't understand. She can't create life with their hands like we can. None of the teachers can."

I nodded. I understood, because I was one of them. Like the children. We were becoming more extinct by the day.

"Anyway, yesterday Miss Rose was absent and they sent a substitute teacher to the class. He didn't know how to work with these children. Every time the children moved their hands or arms to communicate or create life, he shouted at them to stop and be quiet."

"Wow. They didn't even bother sending someone qualified?"

"No. But I was there, so I got to work with them the way I wanted to! The substitute teacher assigned them standard reading from a boring English book. While the kids struggled to read, he fell asleep reading a newspaper! But then I snuck into the middle of the room ..."

"Ooh, you did not!"

"I did! I got all the kids' attention and told them to be real quiet. That I was going to tell them a story ..."

Heart pounding, there I was in the middle of the classroom, substitute teacher sleeping behind me at the teacher's desk.

I got the students' attention and said, "Once upon a time, there was a girl who loved ... what? What kind of fruit did she just LOVE?"

Eric raised his hand and said, "Apple," while a dim form of a Granny Smith apple wobbled in front of him on his small child-sized desk. Noel giggled next to him.

"Good! Apples! She loved apples so much that she would eat one for breakfast, one for lunch, and one for dinner!"

I stretched my arms out with my fingers splayed as wide

as I could make them. With a creaking vibration, a massive tree appeared around me with gnarled roots and hanging leaves. I stood inside the tree, and though it filled the room it did not feel crowded. It became dim and musty and smelled like a forest.

"I'm scared," Noel said. "It's too dark in here!"

I turned to her and smiled. "It is a little bit dark in here! Noel, can you create more light for us?"

Noel raised her hands and made a fist while making a flat surface with her other arm. She set her fist on her forearm, and then slowly raised her fist toward the ceiling.

The room suddenly became much brighter, and sunlight started to stream into the room from above. It became as bright as a sunlit meadow in the middle of a forest.

"Good! That's beautiful, Noel."

"I'm hungry!" said Gwen. She was always hungry.

"Oh, yes, it's almost snack time. Who else is hungry?" I asked the class. Everyone raised their hands around the tree.

"Wow, everyone. Well, who wants some apples?"

Everyone raised their hands even higher. I turned to the tree, lifted my right arm, and cupped my hand like I was going to grab something the size of a baseball from a branch. Apples started to sprout from every limb. Great big apples of all kinds of shapes and colors.

"Go pick one," I said.

All the students got up and scrambled to the tree and grabbed an apple each. Noel got a bright green one, Gwen picked one that was red and pink, and Rui picked a gnarled orange one that was sitting on a root.

Suddenly, at the same moment when a large green apple fell from the tree and plonked on the ground, the substitute teacher crashed to the floor, having fallen out of his seat.

The tree and all the apples disappeared, leaving only the orange one that Rui was holding.

"What's that," the substitute teacher yelled from the ground. "What's that apple?"

Rui's eyes darted back and forth between the teacher and me. I smiled and motioned for him to give it to the teacher. Rui walked up to the teacher and gave him the apple.

"Oh, for me? Why, thank you. That's so thoughtful."

Rui smiled. The class was quiet.

"Wow," I exclaimed. "That's amazing."

A shy smile passed over Meifawn's face. Working with these kids day in and day out took its toll on her. It wasn't the kids who made life difficult, though. It was the adults.

"So what happened with Rui?" I asked. "Did he keep creating?"

"Oh, yes, ever since then he's been plucking apples from everywhere. Under desks? *Pluck.* Behind doors? Inside backpacks? *Pluck, pluck, pluck.* He pulled an apple out of the turtle. That was so funny!"

We glanced down; our feet were intertwined. Smiled at each other.

"But Miss Rose came back today."

"Uh-oh."

"Yeah. She wasn't happy about Rui's apples."

"What did she do?"

"She kept telling Rui to stop playing with apples and to focus on his schoolwork. Every time."

I felt heavy and my heart hurt. "Couldn't she see how important it was to fully express oneself, to create?"

Meifawn shook her head. "But at the end of the class today, Rui and I both winked at each other, said 'See you *tomorrow.*' Tomorrow we will create more."

In front of me, Meifawn put a gnarled orange apple on the table. I smiled and picked it up. It was beautiful.

And delicious.

FAMILY DOG

RAYMOND LUCZAK

[*after Susan Dupor's painting*]

Dogs hold a lot of power. Most of the time they don't realize just how much. They are honest about wanting affection, and we give it to them without thinking about it. But humans asking so nakedly for affection from another? Tank was twelve weeks old when he waddled into Stacy's life ten years ago. She had just turned six, a precarious age when children start to figure out the world isn't what they'd thought it was. She was starting to realize that strangers on the street, usually friends of her parents, behaved differently around her because she wore hearing aids. They over-enunciated their words, remarked what a little sweet girl she was, and smiled and shook their heads at her while talking with her parents.

Her father had a friend who bred English bulldogs on the side, and she had one puppy left and offered him to Stacy's family. Her older sister and brother said, "Awwww!" when they saw the doe-eyed puppy sitting haplessly in the fenced area with his staunch-jawed mother. When Stacy's father scooped him up and carried the puppy to the car, Sarah and Sam argued on the way who'd get to hold the dog on their trip home. She kept saying, "Oh, he's so helpless!" and he kept saying, "He's a boy. He's tough."

Dad said, "Enough of bickering, you two!"

Sarah and Sam turned quiet when Dad looked at Stacy. "You can hold him."

There, on her lap, sat the puppy. His brown eyes looked deep into her eyes, and she knew he would be hers. Didn't matter if others in her family claimed him as theirs. That night Tank was supposed to sleep in her parents' bedroom, but because Stacy never wore hearing aids while sleeping, she wouldn't be bothered by the sound of the clock ticking next to his crate. The sound was supposed to soothe his anxiety of sleeping in a strange place. She watched him from her bed, and even though she was told not to take him out at all, she couldn't take any more of the suspense. She let him out. He sniffed her hands, rolled over onto his back, and waited for her to stroke his chest. A warm buzz-glow filled her body.

Every night at dinner Dad and Sarah joked back and forth, and Mom and Sam kibitzed about his college plans. The lights on them were good, but they tilted their heads when they laughed, or one of them covered her mouth while resting her chin in her hand, or everyone laughed all at once. Faces began to blur as Stacy's eyes tired. Sometimes one of them clapped hands in delight, which distracted her from lipreading. They rarely looked at her or asked if she was following their conversation. Even though she was sixteen, practically a full-grown woman, she was just there. They assumed that she could hear pretty much everything with her hearing aids. It was as if they had expected her to be the world's best lipreader. *No big sweat, right?*

In her bedroom window the shadow of trees rustling in the wind looked like a painting. She could stare at it for hours and feel as if she understood its need to stop trembling for a moment's reprieve from the wind. She was full of shadow, and no one knew it. She has been hiding it for so long that she forgot too much of it inside her could harm.

When Stacy asked for clarification during a quick lull in their dinner table conversations, they always said, "It's too complicated. I'll tell you later." Basking in the glow of laughter with others would always trump any communication need of hers. Sometimes she was lucky to get a five-word summary of what they'd been talking so animatedly about for the last five minutes.

One morning Stacy found it odd that Tank didn't come trotting to her bed to stick his cold wet nose in her face. She got up and looked for him. At first it looked as if he was just sleeping on his big pillow in the living room. She came closer and realized that he was dead. She touched him on the head, and she felt a spark of ice-cold electricity leap into her veins.

After her family finished church, Marie Angstrom, a close friend of Stacy's grandparents, came up to them and regarded them with a beaming smile. "Isn't it so nice, that all of you are so together as a family? Makes me miss those days when my son was living at home."

"Yeah." Dad tousled Sam's head. "Won't be long before he leaves home."

Ms. Angstrom walked closer to Stacy and showed a bit more teeth as she spoke. *Why is it that hearing people think showing more teeth will make it easier for lipreading when it actually makes things worse?* "Stacy, I'm so, so proud of you."

Stacy gave a stiff smile.

"Oh, yes, we all are," Mom said as she gave her daughter a hug. "She's done so well."

"Amazingly well," Ms. Angstrom said. "I don't know how you do it."

"She's no trouble, really."

They talked about Stacy as if she wasn't there. *I might as well be a dog trained to do a few spectacular tricks at the circus waiting for my next treat,* she thought.

Mom said no when Stacy asked for a ride to the Copper Mall where there would be a gathering of deaf and hard of hearing teenagers from all over the area. She hadn't believed her luck when she searched online to see if there were get-togethers for people like her, and there was one for this Friday!

She asked, "Why not?"

"You have enough friends."

"No, I don't. That's why I want to go."

"But you speak so well."

"Mom!"

"It's too far away, and there's that Friday afternoon traffic."

"You've never had a problem picking up Sam at six o'clock after he finishes football practice, so ... ?"

"Stacy. Please. Just because you're deaf doesn't mean that you get special favors."

"When have I ever requested anything special?"

"We'll talk about this later, okay?"

But of course, later never came.

In school she thought about Tank. He always liked to stay under the dinner table. Even though Sarah and Sam tried to tempt him with crumbs and scraps from the table, he never left her side at mealtimes. He would lay on his back and expect her to rub her socked feet all over his chest while she ate. When she didn't do that, he sat right next to her and rested his head against her legs. His heavy breathing sometimes tickled her.

She cried during lunch when she realized what he had been trying to tell her all along: *I'm still here. I'm not forgetting you.*

Mom and Dad said no when she asked if they could get another dog.

Her school was a mile and half away from the Copper Mall. On Friday, Stacy decided to skip the bus ride home and hurry straight to the mall. The trees, filled with orange, red, and yellow leaves, swayed above her. They seemed as excited as she was.

She took the two escalators up to the third floor where the food court, surrounded by fast food joints, was filled with many tables and chairs. At 3:30 in the afternoon, there weren't many people eating there, but she caught sight of a group of teenagers signing at one end. She stopped briefly. She hadn't anticipated that. She expected they would use their voices and hearing aids just like her.

A long-haired girl with barrettes in her hair smiled at her. She waved hello.

Stacy glanced around herself. She was waving *her* over? She wove through the maze of tables toward the other girl and her friends.

Even though the other girl, Marianne, was deaf and used sign language, she was surprisingly easy to understand.

She used a notepad and pen for their conversation, and she introduced Stacy to Eugenie, a girl with a cochlear implant who also knew sign language. She seemed to speak as well as Stacy did, so Stacy started learning about the deaf community. She was amazed that anyone could understand so much about what it was like not to hear well. It was the first time in her life that she didn't feel alone.

It was already nine o'clock by the time they left. The security guard crudely gestured to them and over-enunciated each word directing them to leave as the mall had to close. Suddenly famished, Stacy realized she'd forgotten to buy something to eat there. She couldn't believe how easy it had been to make new friends, and that her hearing aids weren't an issue. She had learned her first signs: "deaf," "hearing," "family." It felt strange to use her hands so openly like that when she'd been taught not to behave differently from anyone. She was indeed *deaf*.

Everyone exchanged text numbers and email addresses, and agreed to meet again the following Friday.

As Stacy rode home in Eugenie's car, the trees, haloed from the lights lining the street, looked as if on fire. *I know I'll catch holy hell tonight,* she thought, *but I don't care*. Tonight she had learned that she was not alone feeling frustrated with her family, and this piece of knowledge had given her an armor of invincibility.

When she entered the house, she was surprised to find Mom, Dad, Sarah, and Sam sitting in the living room. They jumped up and talked all at once when they entered.

Stacy said, "Stop! I can lipread only one person at a time."

Mom said, "Why didn't you call? We were so worried about you!"

"You said you couldn't give me a ride home from Copper Mall, so I went over there on my own and met some new friends."

"What *new* friends?"

"Well, Eugenie—she gave me a ride home. She's deaf like me."

"You shouldn't have—"

"You said we'd talk about this later, but you really didn't want to talk about it at all. There's no 'later' with you, Mom, or anyone! Fuck this shit."

Everyone looked mortified. They'd never heard her use a four-letter word before.

"I'm sixteen years old. I'm not a kid anymore!"

"Stacy! Don't talk back to your mother. Ever!"

She gave her father a dirty look.

Without using her voice, she signed to everyone: "Good night."

Everyone looked aghast. She had been long forbidden to use signs. It was supposed to ruin her speech. *What a joke. They simply don't want me to look different.*

In that moment she realized that silence was her best weapon.

That night she dreamed of weaving through a thick and gnarly forest. The footpath was small, but each footprint indentation felt instantly familiar. Someone else had already walked in her shoes. Knowing that others ahead had paved her way to them filled her with joy. She no longer felt afraid of getting lost here. Everywhere she looked exploded with countless shades of green. Lichen, plastered against the tree bark, dribbled down with pastel hues. Birds of many kinds darted in and out, each wing a needle sewing the fabric of rustling branches. The strain of misunderstanding left her shoulders, and she felt light as a sparrow.

⁂

The next day was Saturday, which meant lasagna night. She made garlic bread with a little bit of parsley sprinkled on top. It turned out perfectly with a hint of brown on the crust.

As Dad doled out a helping for each person, everyone started yammering as before. Sam's guidance counselor had recommended that Sam apply to yet another new college, and Sarah had learned two new songs in cheerleading practice earlier that day.

Stacy could not take any more of this. Being with hearing strangers who didn't know anything about deafness was one thing, but her family should've known better. They would already know how to accommodate her. Stacy said, "Hello?"

No one seemed to hear her amidst their babble.

She raised her voice. "Hello?"

Sarah turned to her. "What?"

"I'm here. Don't ignore me when you're talking with each other."

Sarah rolled her eyes.

"Wow," she nearly shouted. "I didn't realize that I'm too much work for you."

Dad said, "What's going on?"

"Can you please look at me when you're talking with each other so I can lipread?"

"Oh," Sam said. "That would feel so ... weird."

"What's weird is that I have to keep asking you."

"It's those ... deaf friends of yours, is it?" Mom asked. "They're a bad influence on you."

"Not really. I want to feel included here."

"Stacy," Mom said. "Not everything we say is important."

"Shut up, then."

Dad gave her a cold stare. "Don't. Ever. Talk. That. Way. To. Your. Mother."

"Don't. Talk. That. Way. To. Me. I. Am. Deaf!"

Mom and Sarah gasped, and Sam tried to hide his laughter.

She stood up and left the table.

Stacy was surprised when neither Mom nor Dad asked to come into her room for a sit-down talk later that evening. Maybe they had carried on as before, speculating about her growing insolence. She tried to sleep, but it was difficult. Her head buzzed with the question of how she would be punished. But she managed to fall asleep.

In the fog of dawn she was jolted by a cold but familiar sensation on her face. She turned to see what it was. The ghost of Tank was nudging her awake. He licked her forehead once and trotted to her bedroom door. He wanted to be let out of her room. She followed his ghost as she walked down the steps to the kitchen where everyone was making breakfast and chattering happily among themselves.

"Good morning."

Everyone turned to look at her. They yelped in shock when they saw Tank's ghost standing near her.

"Tank! Is that really Tank?"

The bulldog, wagging his tail, looked up at her with askance. He had always loved running to each person for a big hello. She had missed the way his thick paws oomphed on her thighs when he greeted her after school.

She nodded consent.

He waddled to each one and jumped up to their thighs as if to ask for a hello-pat on his head. Blue lightning sparked between them. He moved from one person to another so quickly that no one had time to react to what happened next. Stacy was flabbergasted when each person poofed into an ugly mutt. Her family was now a pack of dogs with no discernible features of a certain breed. She couldn't tell which one was Mom or Dad or Sarah or Sam. Confused and unused to walking about on four legs, they whimpered. They stumbled toward Stacy, but she said, "No, you stay right there." She turned off her hearing aids and texted her new friends to come on over now for an all-day gathering at her house and spread the word. Every deaf person in the area was more than welcome to drop by as long as they brought some food.

Everyone commented on how adorable the dogs were in their own way.

Stacy told them that she'd found them at the local shelter the day before.

"Nice," a guest said. "Where's the bathroom?"

Stacy saw the look of confusion in these dogs: *Who are these strangers coming into our house? Why aren't we using our voices?* They were lost from trying to follow all the hands and wondering why these people were suddenly laughing so hard. Were they poking fun at their predicament? Not at all. But Stacy didn't say anything to reassure them. Each time a mutt came up to her, as if to demand an explanation, she brushed it away. "Not now. Later." She returned her attention to her new family, serving them microwaved leftovers and making lots of lemonade.

Later that night, with the four dogs clustered on the floor around her bed, Stacy dreamed of finding at last a large clearing roofed with generous shade after walking hours through the heavy-misted forest. In that sweet twilight her people, having long dispensed with hearing aids and cochlear implants, sat on fallen logs around a fire and signed with each other, telling each other war stories about their own hearing families. Sitting and resting among their feet were mutts of every size and color. Every so often during their conversations, they commanded their dogs to leap onto their laps for a deep hug and looked into the eyes of their dogs as if to say: *I'm still here. I'm not forgetting you.*

DREADED SILENCE

A. M. MATTE

I'm never sure what to do with myself when I first materialize. I wonder if I should strike a pose. Or find a suitable vantage point from which to perch.

In that nondescript living room, with a drab couch at one end and an abandoned piano at the other, my choices were slim. So it was fortunate that what I really felt like doing was to move and sway to the music in my head.

It was part soft, melancholy tune, calling for slow, languid movement, punctuated by an occasional twirl, and part rugged beat requiring significant exertion and a steady stomping for full effect. Lost in my dancing, I didn't notice my mission as she shuffled into the living room.

It was the beeping of the telephone that alerted me to Van's presence. I whirled around at the sound and took in her appearance—a rank and tattered robe, bags under her eyes, coffee mug in one hand, cordless telephone in the other. Of course, she didn't know I was coming; otherwise I like to think she would have spruced up a little.

The telephone was pressed to her ear. She listened, took a deep breath, and hung up. She set the telephone on the dusty piano in front of her. I watched her staring at it. Since she wasn't busy anymore, I thought it would be best to start the conversation.

"I'm no Terpsichore, but sometimes I like to expand my reach a little bit," I confided. "But let's get to the reason I'm here. I'm so excited about working on this with you. It's about time it was finished."

Van slowly reached for the telephone on the piano, dialed, listened, then hung up, tears in her eyes. I cringed as she thumped the mug onto the piano next to the telephone she'd abandoned a second earlier. She turned, fetched a bottle of cognac from a cabinet, and poured a hefty dose of liquor into her coffee.

"You're not fooling anyone with that," I told her. "Even your Mrs. Desai from across the street has noticed. She understands, maybe, but she noticed. She's worried about you." Van took a big gulp from her mug as I added, "I am, too."

She picked up the telephone again, dialed, listened, hung up. I had to intervene.

"You know he won't answer," I said softly.

She whimpered and hid her face in her hands.

"I'm sorry," I said.

She took a breath and wiped her tears away. She attempted a smile.

"Oh, good! That's the spirit."

I was encouraged, until she looked at her mug and sighed. She picked up the telephone, and I began to get impatient. It usually doesn't take them so long to perceive me. I tried again.

"Maybe if you did something else for a change? That's why I'm here."

She dialed, listened, hung up. She picked up her mug and reached for the bottle.

"Maybe if you *drank* something else for a change ..."

Van put the bottle down and I felt a new hope surge in me. I thought she was finally with me. But she returned to her automatic gestures, picking up the bottle to pour more liquor into her mug.

I almost gave up.

"It's too bad, because ... it really needs your help. It's not finished. And we're so close! If you could just ..."

She picked up the telephone again and—I don't know what came over me—I snatched the receiver out of her hand. Hardly the delicate first impression for which I was aiming.

It worked, though. I wasn't invisible anymore.

"What the *hell*?!" she shouted. "What—who the hell are you?"

She was backing away from me, frantically looking around her, I suspect for a weapon. She picked up the liquor bottle and brandished it.

"Get the hell out of my house!" she demanded.

Not my best manifestation.

"No, you don't understand ..." I started.

"I said—"

"I'm here because of Sergueï!" I interrupted.

She froze, arm above her head.

"What?"

"I'm sorry. It's not my habit to manifest myself this way. I got impatient. I couldn't wait for you to notice me on your own."

She looked confused and forgot her fear. I like to think it's because I'm a calming presence, but it was probably due to how much she'd had to drink.

"What? How long have been here?" She set the bottle down. "You knew Sergueï?"

I attempted to explain. "Sergueï and I had a ... a very

intimate kind of relationship." I watched as her face registered surprise.

"Oh. I—I didn't know."

Her prolonged shock worried me. This wasn't going as I planned. "Are you all right?"

She ignored—or didn't hear—my question. "How long?" she asked.

"Pardon?"

"How long did you two ... know each other?"

I laughed.

"Oh, forever!"

She mulled over my answer. I didn't understand what was bothering her so much.

"Oh ... What's your name?"

"Euterpe," I replied with a swish of my dress. "I'm pleased to meet you."

She didn't say anything. I understood. I have that effect on people. My presence overwhelms them—they are thrilled, energized and debilitated at the same time. When they recognize me for what I am, they are relieved, ecstatic, *inspired*. That's the point. That's why I come. That's how I help. But with this mission, it wasn't the same. She wasn't responding as she was supposed to. Where was the elation, the rapture? I felt the sting of her indifference. I tried again.

"I didn't mean to surprise you. I'm usually much less ... obvious. But I was thinking maybe you'd want to see this. Get your opinion. You are a music teacher, after all; we have that in common."

"You teach, too?"

I smiled, fished out a dozen precious sheets of music from my bodice and handed them to her.

"Something like that," I said.

She read the music. I could hear it in her head. I knew she liked it. Good.

"Mm-hmm. Strong, melodic, not too complicated ... Why show me? This yours?"

"Not entirely ..."

She gasped. One hand clutched at her throat. She understood. "It's *his*, isn't it." She discarded the music brusquely and the pages fluttered to the floor. "That's a mean trick."

"It's not a trick!" I protested. What was I doing wrong? I dreaded having to explain to my sisters, if it got any worse.

"Coming in like this, who asked you?" she continued. "I'm trying to get through this and you just show up here ..."

"I'm trying to help ..."

"How is this supposed to help anything?"

I had to try a different tack. Draw on my extensive experience. Speak from my heart.

"You're right. I haven't been clear and I can see that this is upsetting you. Let me rephrase. I need *your* help."

"Why should I help you? I never even knew about you!"

I shook my head. It was simply that she didn't remember me. A difficult part of the job. Whenever I show up, it's like the first time for them, no matter how many times I visited them before.

"I think you should leave," she stated.

That would be the worst thing to do. I decided I'd have to see this mission through no matter how long it took. I stayed the course.

"No, you have to listen to me. It's important ... It's for Sergueï."

I picked up the discarded sheet music and glanced at it fondly. I knew it so well already, no matter how new it was. I shook the sheets of paper near her face. "Like you said: it's beautiful. But it's not finished. He was working on it when ..."

She looked at me dispassionately. "When he was killed, by an idiot drunk driver. Say it: when he was killed."

"When he ..." I stopped.

"Hard, eh?" Van said, more a statement than a question.

I nodded. "It always is. So many like him who met their demise before their work was done. Well, you know. Wolfgang, Franz, Gustav, Giacomo, Jacques, Jimi ..."

"*... Death, on this occasion, was stronger than art*," she said, quoting Toscanini about Puccini's unfinished *Turandot*. She glanced at the sheet music and continued. "We played some of it at his funeral."

"I know."

"His friends and my friends, they were all there. They said it was beautiful."

"It was."

"You were there?"

"In a sense."

"I don't remember you," she said defensively. She looked me up and down, as if trying to trigger a memory. "I would have remembered you."

"I'm easily forgotten once I've gone."

It's true. I have helped countless men and women discover an inner beauty and I rarely get credit for it. I spend endless nights talking them from the brink of desperation and disaster, I restore courage and conviction and confidence and literally fill the world with music, but I don't get much thanks. It was harder, in the beginning, when the art was new. I'm used to it, now. The real reward is never being without songs in my head. Acknowledgement —or lack of it—doesn't change how I feel about my calling. It feels ... divine.

Van took the sheet music from my outstretched hand. "That was the last time I listened to or even looked at anything he composed. I can't bear to listen to his music, now—any music, from any of my students; it reminds me too much of what I've lost."

I picked up the telephone.

"Then why keep calling?" I asked.

She took a long, drawn-out breath before answering.

"For his voice. The sound of his voice on the answering service. I've been paying his cellphone bill."

"The sound of his voice. Rather than silence. The sound of *him*."

She nodded, then rested her head in her hands, rocking slightly, to and fro.

"... his music ..." I continued. "His music ... his voice."

She stopped moving. I heard what I rarely hear: a pregnant silence. After a time, she looked up at me and I knew I had reached her. I nodded encouragement, almost too eagerly.

"His voice ..." she echoed.

"Yes ...?"

We were so close, I could barely breathe. She took the telephone from me, dialed, listened. She almost hung up, but she hesitated, and I could tell I had finally gotten through to her.

"... Honey?" she said into the telephone, stifling a sob. "It's Mom. Honey? I love you so much. So much. So much I can hardly stand it. I miss you. Too much. And I wish I could hold you in my arms, and kiss you and make it all better. I don't know how come I can keep living without you. You are my love, my darling, my precious, my everything. And you had so much going for you. So much to live for. I can't believe you were cut down in your prime, when you had so much more to give, so much more to create. I am so proud of you. I love what you've done with your life. I'm so proud that I was able to influence you, even just a little, to pursue music and composition as a career. You surpassed me with everything you've learned and accomplished, and I wish you were here so I could tell you again. I love you, and I'm so proud of you. And ..."

She looked at me gratefully. We shared a smile through our tears.

"And I've met your friend. And, if it's okay, we're going to finish it. Because it's so good. It's so beautiful. And I'm going to do my best to finish it the way you would have. I hope you'll be proud of me, too. I miss you, honey, and I love you. More than I can say ... Bye."

My work was done. She was inspired.

Van hung up the telephone and stared at it for a time. I disappeared, but I hovered for a few seconds more.

"Do you think you can help me with this?" she asked.

She looked around, but had already forgotten what she was looking for. She picked up the sheet music and began to hum its tune. She went to the piano, lifted the fall to uncover the keyboard and started to play.

I dematerialized to the sound of the memory of Van's son.

THE VIBRATING MOUTH

JOHN LEE CLARK

It is a tragedy that in the twenty-first century we find ourselves in the same baffling situation we have been in since 1816, when Laurent Clerc sailed for America to establish our first school. He found its shores overrun by human-like creatures that did not speak. Clerc called them the Vibrating Mouth because he observed that spittle flew from their lips. He taught us about them, warning us that they would sometimes capture us and hold us captive, tying our hands and forcing us to vibrate at the mouth.

At the hearth in his and Eliza's home, he would terrify the little ones with descriptions of their idolatries surrounding the vestigial organs at the sides of their heads. "Beware, my children," Clerc would say, "you too possess the same organs. Though they worship their own organs, yours they positively crave. Their thirst is unquenchable. I have seen with my own eyes children like yourselves dragged away to have their organs stabbed with long needles. I have seen them pour into the holes gall mixed in goat's blood. Oh, far better for you if they cut off your organs and set you at liberty, but they will not, they will not!"

Two hundred years later, the Vibrating Mouth have grown to be less outwardly monstrous. In fact, many are quite friendly, and we have had abundant opportunity for observation. One of our traditions is to tell the story of our first encounter. I don't actually remember mine, but my mother loves to tell it for me. It was my first day of school, and a bus was to pick me up. But, for a reason that will shortly present itself, she did not trust the bus driver. So she got in our car and followed the bus. When I stepped out at my school, I was surprised to see her. She asked me if I was all right. I said that I was. "But," I had added, "the bus driver forgot to talk!"

My mother laughed and explained that the bus driver was a Mouthie, so of course it couldn't talk. From that day on, as the story goes, I patted the poor thing on its back whenever I got on or off the bus. I do remember doing that to many other Mouthies. After many encounters, I became something of an expert. Once, out of a perverse adolescent curiosity, I even kissed one. Its lips were soft, but when I reached for one of its hands, its dumb, stilted fingers brought me back to myself and I fled.

Not that they are easily avoided. There are 330 million of them in the United States alone, more than there are of us humans in the whole world. There are billions of them on our planet. Although many of us consume meat with relish, we cannot bring ourselves to eat them, so near to us in appearance are they. Besides, they are often more valuable alive, for they are immediately below us in the food chain, passing up to us much of our food from their farms and fisheries. We also find it convenient to live in some of the buildings they are clever enough to construct.

But it is also true that they are a nuisance, and their staggering sway over everything means we must live with many things that do not agree with us. Fortunately, most of them ignore us, and we are free to do as we please. However, we are much troubled by a certain subspecies of their race that dress themselves in long white coats. In recent decades, these have made a flourishing sport of stealing human babies in order to shave their heads, drill holes into their skulls, and insert something. The idea is that it would cause a perfectly normal infant to descend into mouthing.

We tried to stop these outrages, but swarm after swarm of them would swallow us up, extricating our children from our grasp. There is no logic to their practices. They permit some of our children to attend our schools in peace at the same time they compel others to sit mute all day, vibrating at the mouth in their crude, prison-like imitations of our schools. Most bizarre of all is the taking of our children's hands to their throats while holding up pictures of cows and pigs and hot dogs and ice cream. Whenever one of our children brays at one of these pictures, the Vibrating Mouth go into frenzies.

It is the peculiar way with these creatures that they engage in such rituals without ever accepting any of our babies as one of them. Instead, they send them back to us, often many years later, after they've tired of toying with their mouths. Every year we receive thousands of damaged and traumatized survivors. Thanks to our powers of patience and love, we are often able to teach them to speak, think, and act once again as human beings.

But sometimes we cannot. The problem is that some of them are so damaged that they don't want to be cured. In such cases, the drill had gone in too deep. Some of them commit suicide. We should steal back our own, to save them from the terrible fate of becoming a *thing.* Think of it—to be able only to vibrate, never knowing the heights of poetry or the joys of human connection! But we are outnumbered, and stealing is an abnormal, vibratory act. Our elders also remind us that no human being has ever been the cause—unlike the Vibrating Mouth—of wars, massacres, famines, and such brutalities we have not the words to describe.

Yet we cannot let the Vibrating Mouth get away with their blood sport. Even if they overwhelm the world as a silent, alien majority, we must change the situation. And it may be changing. We have long known that they could be taught to speak, but it was not until recently that we made their rehabilitation one of our primary enterprises. At this stage, we train 500,000 Mouthies annually. Most never get to sing as we do, to take our breath away or bring tears to our eyes, but they almost invariably behave better once they develop a greater awareness of their limited faculties.

Perhaps if enough of them were thus elevated, they would learn that their vast numbers do not entitle them to destroy our world. For that is what these mutes are doing with their old unquenchable thirst, shaving off forests and mountains, drilling even at the bottoms of oceans, and inserting everywhere unspeakably foul wastes, all as though Earth itself were but the head of a human infant. They have succeeded in making it vibrate with increasing violence, but we know they will never embrace it as their home. They might place it under our care, but will our world still have the desire to be restored?

Or will they have gone too far?

GHOSTLY DEMANDS

MARSHA GRAHAM

"This is the tenth call this week, Mira," Francine said, hand on her hip. "Why aren't we getting a handle on this? People are being terrorized by those ghosts!"

Francine Starkis, the sassy retired Boston Police Department detective standing before me, is my boss. She's the face of the private investigation firm Bay State Investigation Services, or BaSIS for short. Massachusetts has an oversupply of names that include the words "Bay State." Every other thing is Bay State this or that.

It also has an oversupply of laws, rules, and regulations. One of those pesky regulations requires private investigators to have law enforcement backgrounds. That's why the Guild of Light Mages hired Francine. Being Miranda Hunter, Mage of Boston, doesn't cut it, so Francine's the boss. My mage partner, Nigel Bley, and I are her minions—sort of—along with my hellhound, Lilit. Francine handles skip tracing, spousal stakeouts, and the like. Nigel and I handle things that go bump in the night—or the day, in this case.

Now, roughly a week since we got our first report, the mundanes were screaming for better answers than "We'll look into it." Our reputation was on the line. I'd sent Nigel out to look for evidence of human pranksters, although it didn't seem likely a mundane could make women's shoes walk by themselves. But, really, how much of a problem was that?

"When I went there, the cemetery was peaceful as dreaming trees," Nigel said. "Except for Buster's overalls."

"It's limited to the Holiness burying ground, because we're not getting calls about other cemetery hauntings."

"Well, at least none of this nature."

True. There were hauntings at all cemeteries; most people just didn't see ghosts. What was allegedly going on at Holiness was a whole new level of spook central, if I took the reports at face value.

"We could hire a medium. Maybe Phoebe Gladstone is available."

"Hello, you two! What are we going to tell these people?" Francine demanded, brandishing a handful of pink message slips.

"Say we're working on it." I shrugged. Honestly I'm not into helping people deal with being pranked by ghosts, or more likely, by another human. I'd sent Nigel out. I'd have told Flanagan, my police cohort in paranormal crime, but it really wasn't Special Investigations Unit material and it would have added to the number of people bugging me for answers. The last thing I needed was a control freak micro-manager cop on my hands.

"I suggested spending the day there with Mrs. Melville, the manager of the burying grounds who is getting the brunt of the problems," Nigel said. "She agreed to meet me. Workers who got totally freaked are out on sick leave."

"They're all people associated in one way or the other with the cemetery," Francine said. To my annoyance, she started waving the pink phone messages in my direction, as if I'd lost sight of them. I wanted to reach out and snatch them out of her hand, but then they'd be mine to deal with. "There have been a few visitors who observed the ... um, events."

"Such as the pair of high heels marching around with no one in them?" I asked. Apparently, that hadn't gone over so well with the daughter of one of the dearly departed.

"The poor woman had a panic attack. They had to call an ambulance," Francine said with a shake of the slips. "Surely that's proof!"

"It's proof that she had a really bad day. We don't know this woman, or how stable she is." I sighed and rubbed at my face. Did this woman really see an office worker's high heels head for the fence without anyone in them?

"And what about—"

Sometimes one has to interrupt Francine. I raised a hand. "I've heard about the shoelaces being tied together while the custodian was alone, and how he fell. We all know about Buster and his inability to keep his overalls up. I even know about the toupée, but you have to admit it was ugly before it ended up in a bird's nest."

"For a mage, you're quite the skeptic," Nigel said. Then he chuckled as if I was a youngling, which to him I am. It's a long story about how long the sidhe, even half-sidhe like Nigel, live. I'll tell you that one some other time. Humans call sidhe fairies, but his great-great-grandmother was the original Banshee. "You've been spending too much time with Flanagan."

Yeah, well, Flanagan was hard to avoid, considering the fact we worked together on paranormal crimes that affected mundanes. He hated being demoted to the paranormal task force and took it out on me, as if it was all my fault. No, this was not crime, it was merely weirdness. With me mediating between two vampire conclaves tomorrow, weirdness could wait.

"The backhoe keys could have been a mistake." I said, making my own mistake by saying it aloud. That was all it took to set Francine off.

"Run up a flagpole?" Francine shot back, message slips waving once again. "Really? That's *quite* a mistake!"

"I don't have all the answers," I said. "I don't know why the office smells like hot fudge and then ammonia. I don't know why the phone rings, but the line is dead. What I do know is that I'm spending the entire day tomorrow trying to prevent a vampire war that could tear this city apart." Not to mention end up triggering the Great Reveal if the mundanes got an eyeful and realized vampires existed outside of television shows and movies. I waved a hand at a huge pile of documents on my desk. "You and Nigel could handle the ghost problem."

"I'm not ghost bait! That's your job!" Francine pointed a long red fingernail at me as if to say: *So there!*

"Fine!" I sighed, shuffling papers into an accordion file. *What's a war between two conclaves compared to shoes walking by themselves? Priorities, people!*

Nigel looked thoughtful. "Mira, Mrs. Melville's purse attached itself to the ceiling. Maintenance had to cut the bottom out to get the contents. According to one of the messages, it's still there. Maybe we can find something."

"Yeah, superglue." I grumbled under my breath as I shoved the folder in the bottom desk drawer. "Okay, Nigel, Lilit, let's go to ghost central and see if we can figure out what's happening."

Lilit got up, practically smiling. She knew she was going for a car ride. Hellhound or no, she loves to stick her head out the window like any other dog. I got her some aviator-type goggles, not so much to protect her, but because a couple drivers ran off the road after seeing her red eyes glowing. Being the creature she is, Lilit makes a great companion in areas where there are unquiet dead. Sometimes it's easier to make that critical contact if you bring along a being created in the demonic realms. More people should try it.

Or maybe not.

Let's face it, during twilight or starlit hours, a cemetery is a different place than during the day. At night it can be a gathering place for teens looking to creep themselves out, or a place where those honored dead who haven't moved on can gather to chew the fat. Daylight hours are for the living, when visitors stop by the office for help finding Uncle Benjamin's grave.

It wasn't a long ride to Holiness. Going by the look of the place, the staff wasn't doing such a hot job of maintenance. The main wrought-iron gate was rusty, hanging at an angle. The hedges hadn't seen a clipper for a while, and the flowering shrubs were getting out of hand. The roadway paving was crumbly, with lots of the little snaky ridges that occur when tree roots run just under the pavement. It seemed to me that all the tombstones could use a good buffing up. Or was that up to relatives and friends of the deceased? A good weed whacker visitation schedule seemed overdue. However, the grass was being mowed as we arrived.

Nigel told me Holiness had once been the ritziest cemetery in the area, the final resting place of many noteworthy families. Personally, when I die, I'm more of a burn-me-up-and-shoot-my-ashes-out-of-a-cannon sort of gal, but if I were into being plonked six feet under in an area of supposed eternal rest, I might want it to look kept up. I guess cemeteries fall into disrepair, but usually those are for common people.

We parked near the office and piled out of my old

International Harvester Scout II, affectionately called the Beast. Buster, the lawnmower guy whose overalls kept heading south, was mowing. With that long-legged, ground-eating stride of his, Nigel took off to talk to him. Fortunately, Buster used a riding mower, so we were not treated to all the splendor of his nudity. The overalls bunched up around his waist, while Buster's dirty, sweaty Patriots t-shirt covered his ample torso.

I walked to the office. The door was locked, but the lights were on. I peered into a window and yup, that looked like a bright red, now-bottomless handbag stuck to the ceiling. *Oh, what the heck.* I walked over to the door, pulled some energy from the unruly landscaping, and sent it to the lock. *Clack!*

Stepping inside, I had to admit it felt off. There was a crackle of energy in the air, and it wasn't anything I'd pulled up. I looked around. There was an old cuckoo clock on the wall, either broken or needing a windup, with a motionless little lumberjack mounted in front. Other than the normal office stuff like business cards, brochures, maps, and such, nothing seemed out of place except the stopped clock and dangling pocketbook.

I wasn't in the best of moods. Instead of preparing for the mediation session, I was in a cemetery office contemplating a ruined handbag stuck to a ceiling. *All rightie then.*

There are benefits to being tall. I often don't need a stepladder. Pulling a side chair away from the desk, I stood on it and examined the purse. It was almost embedded in the ceiling—by its top, not the strap, and with no trace of glue. I tried wedging my fingers under it and got nowhere, then grabbed it with both hands and yanked hard enough to lift myself up into the air a bit. The pocketbook ripped, but the part adhered to the ceiling stayed stuck. It would have been a great glue commercial, had glue been involved. Just when I was about to go magical, Nigel walked in with Lilit and Mrs. Melville, a middle-aged woman in a red dress that matched the purse.

All hell broke loose.

The business cards on the desk shot up like a bungled card trick, whapping rapid-fire into the ceiling. I ducked under a shower of card stock, hands raised to make sure none of those corners hit me in an eye. The cuckoo clock started cuckooing and the little woodsman started chopping away like mad. Maps fluttered around the room like enormous leaves in a high wind. The pocketbook came down off the ceiling and went after the woman in the red dress. She screamed, and Nigel grabbed the demented sack of torn leather out of the air. It struggled free of him. Lilit went after the flapping pocketbook, leaped, caught it like a good canine athlete, and started shredding it with her dagger-like hellhound teeth.

Why the hell hadn't I been ready for bear when I went in here? Because I didn't believe them, that's why. Argh! When would I learn?

My defensive runes were now fully engaged. If it was dark out I'd be glowing. Since it was daylight, I only shone in shadow unless I was supercharged. I focused on the blubbering woman in red. Jumping down, I grabbed her and shoved her out the door, putting myself between her and the cyclone of destruction. As we crossed the threshold, the cards settled to the floor, the cuckoo clock ground to a halt, the lumberjack took a break, maps fell out of the air, and the shredded strips of pocketbook stopped creeping around the floor.

Okay, this was officially hair-raising. *What was she doing, sneaking out to pee on some ghost's grave?*

Nigel and Lilit came out. She looked triumphant and

victorious over the strip of red leather hanging out of her mouth. Captain Nigel of the Obvious tipped his head at the building. "I'd say that's proof of a haunting."

"Ya think?" I gave it a second to sink in. "We need Phoebe." I scrolled through my phone contacts. I don't do poltergeists, ghosts, or other unquiet spirits unless they manifest in a way I can interact with them. Phoebe is the real deal.

Nigel went to comfort the terrified woman, who was huddled behind my SUV. I wondered why Buster only had his overalls come undone, and some other guy's toupée ended up in a bird's nest, but that woman had a shitstorm raining down on her head.

So who did she piss off?

Phoebe answered, her usual cheery self, and said she would be over "quick like a bunny." Excellent. Phoebe liked paying gigs, because most of her medium work didn't make her any money. She was a ghost magnet. When I'd first met her, discarnate beings were hounding her day and night, trying to get in touch with friends and family. (There needs to be a social media outlet for spirits, maybe Ghostbook or Spookspace or something.) I'd created a bespelled amulet to give Phoebe respite from ghostly demands. When she took it off to take a shower, they'd ambushed her—the dead can be demanding. So that she wouldn't have to wear it all the time, I'd gone over and ghost-proofed her house.

Her life partner and driver, Ethan, had all the psychic sensitivity of a mud turtle, and was the perfect sidekick for her. He waited beside the fence while she walked in, all smiles, since she could be on a payday in the making.

Were there ghosts out here with us? No clue, but Buster was not getting any nuder, and there were no flying purses, or empty high heels, or keys clanking from the flagpole. There she was, the most powerful medium in the Northeast present and accounted for with bells on. Real bells. Phoebe has this thing with fairy bells. Drives Nigel nuts, but he's too polite to tell her.

Since too many mages, ghost-whisperers, energy workers, and cooks spoil all sorts of things from spells to soups, Nigel and I took up positions by the fence near Ethan. Lilit, who is an excellent judge of character, bounded out of the gate and up to him looking for a world class doggie ear rub. She got it, of course.

Nigel and I kept an eye on Phoebe as she headed for the office. She's a medium, not a mage, and if things got dangerous, it was our job to protect her. We kept far enough away to stay out of her hair, but close enough to shield her if necessary. I was charged up enough now that my fingernail runes were glowing noticeably even in daylight.

Phoebe started talking, engaging a ghost. Before too long, based on the way she kept turning, it appeared as if she was talking to four or five different beings. From her side of the conversation, her new spirit friends were very upset.

After a few minutes of animated conversation, she came over to us. "Boy, are they pissed!" she said.

"No kidding. Who knew a woman's pocketbook could be a potentially lethal weapon?" Phebes and I ignored Nigel's remark, knowing how lethal a heavy pocketbook could be in the hands of an enraged woman.

"What's happening here is a form of ghostly protest." She gestured around the burying grounds. "Think of it as Occupy Holiness. Look at this place, all run down and tatty. Holiness used to be the place where the Boston Brahmins buried their family members when they ran out of room in the private burying grounds." She gestured about her. "There are cadet branches of the Cabots, Lowells, Bacons, Choates, and Crowninshields interred here. I just met them."

Nigel nodded. "*And this is good old Boston, the home of the bean and the cod, where the Lowells talk only to Cabots, and the Cabots talk only to God.*"

If I rolled my eyes any harder they'd get lodged in my cranium. We were on the verge of having a vampire war in Boston, Nigel was quoting an old drinking toast, and we were in a burying ground—a traditionally Bostonian term for a graveyard–with pissed off ghosts upset about the cemetery being *tatty*? It was a face-palm moment and I scrubbed at my face to shut myself up before I had irate ghosts bombing us with airborne tombstones or something.

"What did they think they were doing?" I asked Phoebe. "Making a fuss so eventually a medium would show up?"

"That never occurred to them. They were simply trying to humiliate the people who shame them and their family members by letting this burying ground turn into a cemetery slum."

I found myself silently counting to ten. Looking at the still quivering woman in red, I reminded myself Phoebe was just representing what her clients were saying. The terms *petty, small-minded,* and *spiteful* floated through my mind. They terrorized mundanes over less than sumptuous surroundings in a graveyard? The place was a little seedy, but it was not a slum.

I suppose if you're a Cabot and only talk to God, maybe that's how they saw it, but to my mind that attitude made them elitist, vindictive snobs. It also begged the question of why they were still here and not off talking to God.

Shaking myself from my reverie, I got down to business. "Nigel, what's that woman's name again?"

"Mrs. Melville."

"That's right. Bring Mrs. Melville here, if you would. We're going to get to the bottom of this." As he left, I looked at Phoebe. “Phebes, please tell me that the dead are not wandering around all the burying grounds looking for wilted flowers to complain about.”

She didn’t look concerned. “Not in my experience. These gentlemen seem to be stuck. They need to go into the light, but until I can help them past their anger it won’t be possible. Realize, in their day this was the Ritz-Carlton of resting places.”

I thought of where my life-partner, daughter, and our family were buried and shook my head. *Don’t judge, Mira.*

By the time Phoebe laid the concerns of her dead clients on the manager of the facility, Mrs. Melville—no relation to Herman, she insisted—was more than ready to do an information dump. “It’s the endowment fund,” she sniveled. “The impact of the Great Recession and the drop in interest rates hasn’t given us enough income to do everything we need to do.”

“You’re running out of money?” Nigel asked. “That doesn’t bode well for the status-conscious ghost.”

“We’ve applied for subsidies, but we haven’t gotten any yet. We’re full, so we can’t sell new plots. We can’t re-use these graves. Unless we get more funds, we will have to cut back on maintenance again.” She took an unsteady breath. “In the worst-case scenario, we’ll have to close.”

I turned to Phoebe. “Go talk to your clients. It sounds as if the staff here are doing the best they can under the circumstances.”

“They’re here,” she said. “They heard. They had no idea. Give us a few minutes.” She walked off to engage once again—client confidentiality and all that.

“You’d think if they were doing an effective haunting they’d have seen the cemetery manager agonizing over the books of business,” I muttered to Nigel, who shrugged.

In the end, Mrs. Melville was immensely thankful, since this meant that the cemetery would go back to its pre-haunting normal. It wasn't as if she hadn't been trying even while being terrorized. Besides being frightened half out of her wits, she was embarrassed about the cemetery's neglect. One of the Cabots decided to hire Phoebe to contact living family members to contribute to the depleted endowment fund. My best guess is that they had some sort of insider information she could present to avoid a call to the fraud squad.

Things were wrapped up here. Francine would be as happy as she ever got; Flanagan would never find out about the haunting, if I was lucky. Nigel and Lilit were hinting at stopping by for a slice at our favorite pizzeria. And me?

I still had to pull off a vampire peace treaty. Just one more day in the life of the Mage of Boston.

THE JOB
MAVERICK SMITH

It was raining. Again.

Green lights flashed and flickered on my belt as my Weather Watcher™ automatically calculated the amount of acidity in the rain and attempted to determine if it fell within the "safe" limits set out in the global environmental standards. Normally, the device made noise too, an awful racket of whirs and clicks. I resisted the urge to push back the hood of my rain slicker and check the volume controls on my BatEar™. Exposing it to the rain would void its warranty. Tia was leading us through the packed pathways of the barrio. Even if my BatEar™ wasn't working properly, Tia's rust red jacket proclaimed her to be one of the Silenco. We would be safe enough from accidental—though maybe not intentional—confrontations. Only the most ignorant person from off-world was unaware of the significance of Silenco red.

As if sensing my gaze, Tia turned to face me and Adam, smiling broadly despite the fact that her obsidian face was streaked with raindrops. *We're almost there,* she signed fluidly. *I'll give our usual spiel once we arrive. You should both stay in the back, especially you, Adam.*

My BatEar™ picked up the vibration as Adam shifted his weight beside me. It appeared the echolocation feature was working even if its manual control seemed to be malfunctioning.

"Did you catch that?" I asked Adam, turning to gauge his reaction. It was always hard to predict how foreign, able-bodied, cis men would react to the barrio born, Silenco, genderqueer Tia taking the lead.

"Yes?" Adam said hesitantly. When I raised my eyebrows at him, he translated Tia's instructions into the national *lingua franca* with its Anglophone roots, which folks from off-world favored.

"Excellent," I said and painstakingly demonstrated how he should sign his acknowledgement and understanding to Tia.

The smile had dropped from Tia's face by the end of my slow practice session with Adam. Her signs were fierce in their descriptors as she gave us directions. I was following her tight black braids around the outskirts of a marketplace when the TextTalk™ slate strapped to my forearm flashed purple, indicating she'd sent me a message.

<*Adam frustrating to work with. Wish we could hire a muscleman who is fluent in sign.*>

<*Me too. I am sorry there was not time to find a more competent hire.*>

The pause that came after my message made me think the connection had failed. TextTalk™ was a locally created technology that ran off a solar-powered relay system. The solar batteries charged during the day so it could run through the night, depending on the equipment's quality. But regardless of the hour the grid was known to fail from time to time.

I was about to use another method to get Tia's attention when a reply popped up on my screen.

<I appreciate the apology. Next time I will take a more active role in the hiring process. In the meantime, being able to work with you every day goes a significant way toward making up for Adam's shortcomings.>

It was unmistakably a compliment, perhaps even a flirtatious one. Ages ago, when we first opened our investigation agency, Tia and I had dated briefly. She decided it was too difficult to mix the personal with the professional and gently ended it. Was she now rethinking her decision?

I must have stopped moving in surprise because Adam walked into me. Ignorant foreigner.

Adam might have listed himself as having special skills, but paying attention to his surroundings was not one of them. Ahead of us, alerted by the proximity alarm at her belt, Tia turned and favored me with a slow unmistakably flirtatious wink before continuing on her way.

I heard the crowd before I saw them, my BatEar™ oddly magnifying their shuffling feet and crying babies. Like Tia, they were clothed in the rich red jackets of the Silenco. The adults spilled over into the street while children kept behind the ivy-covered fence. The adults broke apart from their huddles at Tia's approach. After a moment a woman whose blue tattoos of rank indicated her as the head of the household stepped forward.

The tale she signed was a tragic one judging from the expression on Tia's face as well as her tense replies. Punctuating the conclusion of her speech, the woman made a crushing motion even a foreigner could interpret. Tia nodded, echoed it, and gestured toward the two of us. The matriarch turned back to the huddle of her kin and Tia stamped across the muddy earth to us, her face a thundercloud to rival the ones in the skies above. A particularly hard-hitting case, I guessed. Tia's signs confirmed as much.

The latest missing child was a five-year-old boy, born to Silenco parents, and had been stolen at sunset yesterday. He was a few moons shy of the mandatory hearing tests required by the Ministry of Education. Similar to the other Silenco children who had gone missing lately, he was believed to have some hearing. Because of the commonality, his parents suspected an intermediary had grabbed him with plans to sell him to foreigners who, as rumors went, used the Silenco children for their medical experiments.

It was a familiar tale with a usually tragic outcome, hence Tia's grim face. But our investigative outfit already had a short list of intermediaries we suspected of such dealings. I brought the profiles up on my data pad, discarding two as unwilling to work after dark since their prosthetics required sunlight to function. That was the problem with our resource-poor planet, not even the bad people could afford to import the high-quality technology that ran off non-renewable resources.

Framing the remaining three names in black on a yellow background for easy viewing, I passed the data pad to Tia who signed a quick *thank you* before scanning the list. Selecting from a drop-down menu, she put a grave marker beside one of the names and a question mark beside another. Dead and maybe disappeared. That narrowed our list down to one. Unfortunately he had an entire city to hide in.

It was dusk before we found our target quenching his thirst at a downtown bar. Our muscleman actually earned his salary, escorting him out of the bar and tossing a hood over his head before he could recognize Tia or me. One of the advantages of hiring the ex-military was that when Adam marched our captive through the streets, people edged out of the way rather than crowding him with questions. This fortunate trend held until we reached our destination, one of the rundown properties our firm had purchased for precisely this purpose.

Adam wrenched the hood off our captive once he was strapped into an ancient wooden chair for interrogation. He quailed at the army uniform Adam wore, but it wasn't until Tia, garbed in red, stepped out of the shadows and fixed her angry gaze on him that the man began to talk. And talk.

When the words started to spill from his lips, I stepped forward so Tia could see me, interpreting what our captive said until long after my fingers had grown sore. When he ran out of secrets to spill, I let Adam earn his keep by hooding him again. The three of us stepped into the hall to discuss how this retrieval operation would go.

"The foreign medical company he named is near the port," Adam said unnecessarily. I'd inferred that already without looking at a map. Foreign companies used the buildings nearest the port as warehouses for holding goods before they were shipped off-world. It made sense that the abductors would be holding the kid there. And there would probably be others.

Tia obviously agreed with me because she signed fast and angry, starting her sentence with an insult about Adam's intelligence. For the stake of maintaining relations between colleagues, I didn't translate the insult but instead focused on the logistics of her plan.

We would hire a new muscleman after this case, for certain. There were always unemployed, ex-military types eager to obtain visa permits by working for locals. The alternative was going back to their ruined, war-torn home worlds.

"Tia thinks we should visit the local weapons dealer. Storm the place. Expose the operation and the scientists will scatter like skitters. They know the global government won't look kindly on this affront to their Silenco citizens. I concur."

"As do I," Adam stated, thankfully proving he had read at least one entire document in his life. "What these off-worlders are doing falls outside the Codes and Conventions."

Our outfit made decisions collectively. Now that we knew how we would handle the situation, the question of when still needed to be considered.

Two hours before the port opens, Tia argued. *That way we can catch a few hours' sleep.*

No—

You're exhausted. So am I. We could use the rest.

The sign she used specified the more personal "we." My flying fingers froze before I folded them into fists.

It's too busy this time of night to confront them, Tia added. *Besides, the criminals won't move the kid off-world until the dawn. All ships are grounded during petite-mort.*

I translated the second part of our conversation to Adam just in case, not caring if he'd understood the first, flirtatious exchange. By *petite-mort,* Tia meant the ión storms that raged in the exosfera and mesósfera prevented any light from reaching the ground for several hours after our planet had spun away from our sun. Due to the havoc this played with our communications technology, petite-mort effectively grounded all inter- and intra-planetary craft. Off-world travelers hated the inconvenience, but that was the price they paid to dock here.

"Ok." Adam said after a moment. "In four hours, then. The three of us will meet ..."

At the office. Tia finished his trailing sentence before extending one hand for me to take. My pulse leapt at the open invitation and I almost forgot to translate her last statement before slipping my non-dominant hand into hers.

The two of us conversed one-handed as she led us toward her place. Her suite of rooms were as I remembered them, painted in brilliant bright hues that one of her ex-lovers had scorned as feminine but which I had always understood as fierce. And femme. The owner of the flat, eagerly divesting us both of our clothing as we slowly progressed toward the bedroom, was unashamedly both.

I just want to sleep, Tia told me. *Sleep, skin to skin. Safe. Then go rescue the kid. After we can celebrate. Together.*

I sketched an affirmative, set the alarm to wake us at the appropriate time and set about detaching my BatEar™. I would get it looked at by a technician after this case but in the meantime I needed to put it in some sheltered spot so as not to void its warranty. I opened the bedside drawer in front of me ... and paused.

An extra carrying case for the device was already there, in my favorite shade of purple. I glanced over at Tia's figure on the bed, her mouth open in what I guessed was a snore. Inviting me over for these next four hours was not a decision she'd made on a whim. If she'd gone to the trouble of tracking down a carrying case for this particular BatEar™ model in my favorite color ... well. I felt my cheeks heat as I slid under the sheets with her to spend the next few hours in slumber.

The alarm awakened me, vibrating the bed with an insistent, dissonant pulse that was impossible to sleep through. Tia flicked her fingers through an impressive display of insults before sitting up to slap the alarm off. I gathered up our clothes. While I dressed and laid out Tia's fighting garb, Tia defrosted and heated two FeastsForFightin'™ burritos in her compact cooker. She fetched a very familiar jacket from her front closet. It was one of the two fighting jackets I owned.

I'd left it there during our brief foray into dating and I had never gotten around to asking for it back. Like the one I had at home, the jacket was reinforced to be resistant to blaster fire. The fact she had kept it was more evidence that she had intended to have me over again.

I didn't comment on it, though. I knew better than to talk to Tia before she had her morning caffeine. We ate on the way to the office, only stopping at the all-hours caffeine joint Tia preferred. It was cold during the petite-mort, but her smile as I paid for her purchase warmed my heart like the midday sun.

The muscleman was already at the office when we got there, methodically cleaning and laying out our arsenal. Adam had listed weapons as a specialty, and based on the devices of destruction laid out around him, he hadn't falsified that part of his résumé. And he had some extremely inventive ideas for how we could place them on our persons for maximum maneuverability and accessibility.

Hmm, I remarked to Tia. *Perhaps we should keep this one around after all.*

Her resulting answer was ambiguous. But then it was a conversation we could have after the case was closed, and after we learned if there were any vices or ill habits Adam spent his earnings on.

Tia led the three of us through the darkness of petite-mort, her red Silenco jacket looking almost black when we passed out of range of the streetlights. Few people were foolhardy enough to challenge folks that walked abroad during this, the darkest, coldest part of the night. The port and the area nearby resembled a ghost town during petit-mort as starship captains and crews headed to the entertainment district to mix with the locals.

Once we were there, I shot out the security camera. Adam

unhooked a tube from his belt and used it to spread paste over the door hinges. He repeated the process using another substance from a different tube. The resulting mess began to sizzle and corrode the hinges. Then Adam demonstrated why we had hired him and kicked open the battered steel door.

Tia, brave, bold and beautiful, strode in first, taking out everything—person or 'bot—that crossed her path. Several stunned scientists and scattered 'bot bits later, the muscleman kicked open an unmarked locked door to a sight that made my face taut with anger.

Obviously a place where off-worlders performed their "science" on human subjects, the room was dominated by an ancient repurposed starship seat that had had cuffs for restraints welded on at the wrists and ankles. In the shadows beyond the chair, someone whimpered. My BatEar™ magnified the sound.

Light, I signed. It was Adam who shone a light in the direction I indicated. Perhaps there was hope for him yet. The light moved rapidly over a number of white-clad forms with stubble for hair. I revised my opinion. He didn't move slowly enough for them to sign to us.

Huffing out an angry breath, Tia stepped forward, positioning herself under the blinding light that shone down around the chair. Her bright Silenco jacket was the symbol the abductees had been waiting for. They flowed out of the shadows to surround Tia in a short, silent huddle, fingers moving in the signs for *rescue* and *home* and *safe*.

Tia signed affirmations to them all, then looked over their hands at me. She nodded once, a muscle clenched in her jaw. We had rescued twelve other kids in addition to the one whose family was paying us for the job. Thirteen Silenco kids who would've been lost had we waited any longer.

Tia sent a message ahead. The matriarch's family was waiting when the sixteen of us crested the hill. The moment we did so, the kid was enveloped in his mother's arms. Other members of the clan took turns patting his hand or ankle to reassure themselves of his presence. The other twelve kids were similarly welcomed with hugs and careful repetitions of sign-names. Jubilantly, the crowd escorted us to the matriarch who stood waiting, clutching a brilliant blue purse.

The matriarch kissed Tia on both cheeks before enfolding her in a quick hug. She formally presented her a heavy pouch of money. It sounded like a luxurious amount; because of my BatEar™, despite the folds of the bag, I could hear the clinking of coins from where I stood three paces behind Tia. When she stepped back, Tia made her way over to me, slipping her arm into mine.

The matriarch is happy to welcome the twelve other kids to her home until their kinfolk can be located, Tia said. *She invites us to stay for the celebration tonight. We would be honored guests.*

Honored guests? All of us? I looked over my shoulder for the muscleman. He was surrounded by a crowd of young people of all genders who were patiently demonstrating signs for him to replicate. Tia was still waiting for my reply.

I think that sounds like a splendid idea, I told her. *A fitting way to celebrate the closure of a successful case.*

Her answering smile made the red clothing of the Silenco around me seem dim by comparison. And I knew despite what others might think I had the made the right choice to register as a private investigator. It brought me moments like this, surrounded by community with my lover at my side.

THE CLIMAX

TONYA MARIE STREMLAU

Dec. 14

Dear Mom—

Wanted to let you know that I turned in my last paper today! I'm so excited to be done. Also, I got an email from Prof. Johns today that there's an immediate opening for an English teacher at the Midwestern School for the Deaf. I sent in my application! It's lucky I had my resume and a videotape of my teaching philosophy already done from a class. (: Wish me luck! That would be a much better job than substitute teaching at Clerc Center! The bad news is that if I get it, I can't come home for the holidays because I'll need to pack up and move.

Love,

MJ

Dec. 18

Dear Prof. Johns,

I got the job! Thank you so much for telling me about it and encouraging me to apply. The principal, Dr. Grant, interviewed me by videophone yesterday, and today he emailed me a job offer. I'll start right after New Year's. I'm excited!

Not sure if I'll get a chance to see you before I leave, but I'll be back in May for hooding and graduation. Dr. Grant said I would be able to come back for that. He says he's met you at one of the Deaf Ed conferences. CEASD perhaps? He seems like he'll be a good boss. He's even given me a lead on a place for rent near the school, a basement apartment in another teacher's house.

Thanks again!

Mary Jane Bradford

Dec. 18

Hi Jon,

Thanks for sending the pictures and video tour of your basement apartment. The rent seems reasonable, and it sure will make things easier that you include utilities and WiFi. I will take it! It looks nice. I like how much light it has for a basement apartment. The open living area is so deaf-friendly. You said that when you renovated you installed a built-in visual signaling system. Does that include a visual doorbell? Just trying to figure out what I'm going to need for my new place.

I plan to spend Christmas Day with friends here in D.C., and start driving there the next day. I should probably arrive in the afternoon on the 28th. Let me know if that doesn't work for you.

Best,

Mary Jane

Dec. 28

Hi Mom!

Wanted to let you know I arrived safely. It was snowing

when I got here. Fortunately I made it, but the old Corolla isn't going to cut it here. I guess now that I have a job I can buy a new(er) car that will handle better in the snow. It is pretty here, but cold!

I'm going to get to work putting things away. Jon, my landlord, did a great job designing this apartment. There are built-in bookshelves in the living area, and the bedroom has a walk-in closet with shelves and drawers. Since there are already two stools at the breakfast bar separating the kitchen from the living area, I won't need much furniture beyond a bed and a sofa.

Jon is really friendly. Maybe it's that famous Midwestern thing? He invited me in for coffee when I got here and helped me unload my car. And since I don't have any food and the snow is still coming down, he's invited me to join him for dinner tonight. Isn't that nice?

Love,

MJ

Dec. 28

Jilly—

Missing you like crazy. Tried to FaceTime you, but you must be away from the screen. So will resort to writing! Arrived earlier this afternoon and am as settled in as I can be until I can get some furniture. I just ordered myself a bed—not looking forward to my sleeping bag on the floor tonight. Thank God for the Internet and a landlord who lets me use his WiFi.

Jon seems like he'll be a good landlord, but I so wish you were here to help me figure him out. You'll just have to do it from a distance! So, I'm guessing he's around 45. Gray hair, weathered skin. He teaches history in the high school, and coaches the football and baseball teams. He remodeled this whole house himself, opening up walls in the old farmhouse to make it more open-concept and deaf-friendly. He even wired it all for visual alarms. He's not bad looking for his age: a little beer belly and in need of a haircut that would work with his receding hairline, but he has strong arms and a square jaw and bluish-green eyes.

I can't believe someone like him is living here. This place is really the boonies. What's he doing here? I can't see staying here forever—too lonely. He's got that big Deaf family out in California. I mean, everyone in the Deaf community knows the Princes. Why wouldn't he get a job near them? Does that seem weird to you? If I had a Deaf family, especially in a place with at least one local Starbucks, you couldn't pry me away. Your thoughts?

XO

MJ

Dec. 30

Hiya Jilly—

Happy New Year's Eve Eve! Sure wish I was back in D.C. with you so we could ring the New Year in together. You going to H St.? Looks like I'll be going to a party Jon annually hosts for the local Deaf community. He makes his "famous" chili, and everyone else brings something for a potluck. It will be good to meet some of the other people here.

I've got so much to tell you! Thanks for sharing your thoughts about Jon. I have to say I guess I'm getting used to him. I can't believe how nice he's been. I still wonder about him, and think he's lonely. He made a really nice dinner the night I arrived—pan-fried pork chops and mashed sweet potatoes with vanilla ice cream for dessert. And a bottle of red wine. We talked over dinner for a long time, and moved to his den after to finish off the wine. We figured out a bunch of people we both know. Lots of professors and staff at Gallaudet. Some worked there when he was a student (more than 15 years ago!) and some went to school with him, or he knows them from NAD or other Deaf organizations. Then there are some of his former students who went on to Gallaudet, plus his cousins. And believe it or not, our favorite interpreter (yes, her—the hippie goddess) is his former sister-in-law!

I told him how I got curious about Deaf people and ASL when I saw Deaf people signing in the waiting room at my audiologist's office. He said he couldn't believe I hadn't started signing until I took my first ASL class as an undergrad. I hope the rest of the Deaf community here is as welcoming and not as cliquey as Gallaudet.

We even talked about you. (: Jon asked me why I hadn't gotten a CI when my hearing got worse. But by then I had met you, my first Deaf friend. Remember our many long talks about my doctor's recommendation that I get an implant? You were so patient with my back-and-forth thinking. One of the many reasons I love you!

We talked fairly late. Not sure how late, because I don't even remember going down to my apartment. I guess the driving and unpacking, and the wine, were too much. I must have been really out of it because I didn't even put on my PJs. Just took off my clothes and got into my sleeping bag. And I forgot to lock the door from my apartment to the stairs that connect it to the house. (There's a laundry room I share with Jon at the bottom of the stairs.)

When I finally woke up it was almost 10:00! I ate a granola bar from the care package you sent me off with—the only food I had here! Thank you again for that. The snow from the day before had stopped, but it looked like there were at least six inches on the ground from what I could see from my window. (The basement is really a half basement.

The house is set into a slope, so on the back of the house the basement is at ground level.)

I felt foggy and had a headache, probably from the oversleeping and no coffee, so I took a shower to revive. I just got out and was wrapping myself in my bathrobe when the lights flashed—the doorbell! I figured it had to be Jon. Of course it was him. He held two travel mugs, one of which he held forward as soon as I opened the door. Once his hand was free so he could sign, he told me it was coffee and apologized for interrupting my shower. He said he was heading to Wal-Mart to buy a few things and offered me a ride. That way I wouldn't need to clear snow from my car or worry about the roads. Nice, huh? He came in to sit at the breakfast bar and drink his coffee while I got dressed. A little strange. I guess he just didn't have anything better to do.

At Wal-Mart Jon insisted we shop together since he knew the store layout and could help me find what I wanted. He bought things for his New Year's Eve party, and I got everything on my list, from food to a kitchen trash can. But what is cool is that Jon suggested I look at the furniture and the end result is that now my living area has a futon and reading lamp. I'm sleeping there for now, until my bed arrives! It's a good thing Jon drives a pickup with a shell on the back. Plenty of space to haul things.

Today I went to the county seat to get a driver's license and make my move official. They call it a "city," but you could walk one end to the other in twenty minutes. I know because when I finished, I decided to take a walk to see a bit of the town. Norman Rockwell would love this place. Tidy, well-kept houses, all with their sidewalks cleared of snow. Churches on either side of the courthouse (one Catholic, one Lutheran), a diner across the street. This will take some getting used to, but I definitely don't mind that there was no wait at the DMV.

Hard to believe tomorrow is the last day of the year! Miss you bunches.

XO

MJ

Dec. 31

Hi Mom!

Happy New Year! I wanted to let you know that the kitchen things you ordered for me arrived. Thank you! Now I feel like I have a functioning kitchen. I can see you put a lot of thought into what I might need. Maybe I'll even learn to cook some. Now I'm mostly set up here and have plenty of space for you to stay. (Hint, hint!)

My big news is that I've decided to get a cat. My lease said nothing about pets, so I asked Jon. He has no pets, but he says it is fine. I'll adopt from the county shelter. It's a win-win. A homeless cat gets a place to live and I'll get someone to hang out with.

Jon is having a New Year's Eve party for the local Deaf community. I've been smelling his chili cooking all day. (: It will be good to meet the other Deaf people here. A lot of them work at the school, so I'll be meeting my future co-workers, too. Most of them are staff, though. Jon says most of the teachers are hearing.

Happy New Year!

Love,

MJ

Jan. 4

Jillllllyyy!!!!

It was so good to catch up with you on FaceTime the other day!

Remember your question of if Jon might be interested in me romantically? I think you are right. I don't know why

I didn't pick up on it before. I guess because he's old enough to be my dad and I was looking at him like a dad or uncle. I never thought I would say this about someone so much older than me, but I think I should give it a chance—it is lonely out here, and the younger single deaf men out here, none of them have college degrees. Not that I would hold that against them. Plenty of smart and interesting people haven't gone to college. But the whole community was at Jon's party, and everyone—even the hearing interpreter who is married to the school's deaf third grade teacher—looked pained when they found out I teach English. What did they think I was going to do, tell them their subjects and verbs weren't agreeing? We weren't even using English. Sheesh.

Still, Jon hasn't made a move beyond checking me out and doing things that could just be very neighborly—sharing dinners, picking up my mail, things like that. So we'll see. I'd do anything to be with you right now in D.C., hanging out with a group of smart, educated signing folks and talking politics or philosophy or even sports.

And maybe I'll feel less lonely now that I've got a cat! Yes, you read right. I went to the animal shelter today and brought home a gorgeous female orange tabby. The shelter assures me she's had all of her shots and has been fixed. Not that I'm planning to let her roam outside, but cats do get out. I'm still trying to decide on the name. Her orange color has me thinking Mandy (for Mandarin, like Mandarin oranges) or Canty (for cantaloupe). What do you think?

XO

MJ

Jan. 6

Dear Prof. Johns,

I started my new job today. The teacher who quit in

December left behind complete lesson plans for the rest of the quarter, so that will help ease me in. I also need to start planning for next quarter. I'm most excited about the senior class's upcoming unit on the short story. I get a lot of leeway to pick which stories.

This job will be a challenge. I'm grateful for your support. There really isn't any here. Some of the hearing faculty sign so badly I can barely understand them—am pretty sure most of the students can't understand them. And then they sit in the faculty lounge at lunch complaining about how their students don't pay attention to them. I can't believe this is still going on today, but am hoping I can make a difference. My students definitely seemed glad to have a signing Deaf teacher. Mark, one of my seniors, even stayed after school today to help me figure out the classroom tech.

I also have some support from my landlord, who teaches history. He graduated from the Education Department at Gallaudet, too, but I think well before your time. I never thought I'd miss having to write papers for class, but I miss the people that come with grad classes—professor and classmates alike.

Best,
Mary Jane Bradford

Jan. 6

Hi Mom!

I started my new job today. Had a quick meeting with the principal before school and met my classes. Tonight I'm reviewing the lesson plans I inherited. I'm sure Mandy will help me. She's curled up next to me. I can feel her purr every time I reach over and scratch her ears.

Mandy gave me a good scare early this evening. I went out to run some errands, and when I came home, I couldn't find her anywhere! I was sure she was in the apartment when I left, but I looked high and low, and no cat. Not under the bed (which arrived two days ago!), or under the futon, or in the closet or any of the kitchen cupboards. And yes, I opened them all. You never know if a cat might figure out how to open a cabinet door and hide inside. So I had to conclude that she had somehow gotten out, and I was so mad at myself. I was trying to figure out what to do, and got out my laptop to start making a flyer in case someone found her. Then the doorbell lights flashed—Jon was outside holding Mandy. He said he found her curled up on top of his truck. I was so happy I gave him a kiss!

Love,

MJ

Jan. 8

Jill,

Hoping you have some advice for me. I've been getting anonymous love-letter emails (from a Yahoo account) from someone who signs off with "Your secret admirer." This person definitely knows who I am. He makes comments about what I am wearing, how I fix my hair, etc. That alone would be disturbing, but from the things he says it seems like he also has watched me at home and somehow has read my email. He also knows what I'm doing at work, with comments about my teaching. I'm really afraid it might be this kid in my senior class, Mark. He's known on campus as a computer genius and has a scholarship for next year to MIT; and he only just turned 16! I hardly need to tell you that makes him a star here. I don't have any proof it is Mark, but I think he's the only one capable of this. And he does watch me intently in class.

If I accuse him, I'll make enemies whether I'm right or

not. I've got to do something, though. Whoever it is says he watches me while I'm sleeping and plans to join me soon. Maybe I should have gotten a dog instead of a cat.

Do-do?

MJ

Jan. 10

Jilly—

I wish you were here. I just got back from the vet, where I had to have Mandy put down. I'd try to get you on FaceTime, but it is so late. I stayed after school to meet with two students who want to revive the school newspaper and needed a faculty sponsor. When I got home, Mandy was lying in front of my door, covered with blood. I wrapped her in some towels and rushed her to the vet. There was so much blood I couldn't really tell where it was coming from, though it looked like most was from her chest area. I thought maybe she got caught on a barbed wire fence. When the vet examined her, though, she said that someone had cut off a heart-shaped piece of skin and fur. What kind of a creep does that?

The vet called the police, and we made a report. The cops asked me who might have done it. I told them about the emails I've been getting. They asked me to give them the emails. They said it is really hard to identify someone using an anonymous email account because companies won't reveal client information and even fight court orders. I told them that I thought it might be someone from school, maybe a student. I didn't name Mark, but if the cops go and ask around school his name is sure to come up as someone with the tech skills to hack my accounts. Plus, I can't be the only person who thinks he is creepy. Jon offered to let me sleep up in his place, so I'll probably go up later. There's no way I will feel safe enough here to sleep tonight.

I feel so damned guilty. Mandy must have gotten out when I was leaving this morning and juggling all my crap for work. I can't believe she is gone. The more I think about this, the more I'm freaking out. There's some psycho here!

MJ

Jan. 11

Mom,

I know you are worried. Me too! Thanks for FaceTiming with me so late last night. You always make me feel better. I asked Jon to install a motion-activated light outside of my door and add a deadbolt lock. He'll do that this weekend. Jon is restoring a bit of my faith in humanity. He is going to bring me dinner tonight so that I won't have to bother with food or thinking about what to make. He will just reheat some of his chili but that's a lifesaver since I was barely functioning today. I don't know how I got through the day at work.

I really miss you. Come visit soon?

Love,

MJ

Jan. 12

Jilly,

Thank you so much for sending the flowers for Mandy. I wish you could have met her. I had her cremated, and now have the ashes in an orange urn to keep with me forever. I can't believe how quickly she was taken away from me, but I hope that I made her last days better even with the horror of her last day.

I wonder if she came into my life to bring me closer to Jon? When he stopped by to check on me today, he leaned in to kiss me. That turned into a long makeout session. Maybe this is the wrong time to start something like this, but I need the comfort. The police tell me they are investigating. I know they questioned Mark because he was absent from my class and I got a message from the front office to give him an excused absence. It was nice not having him there staring at me the whole period. I guess the cops don't have enough evidence yet, because there's still no arrest. I'm afraid they don't see the death of a cat as a high priority.

Hugs.

MJ

Jan. 24

Jilly,

Work is going pretty well though it's been hard to focus. We've started the new quarter, so now I've got my own lesson plans. I like that better—it really feels like the classes are mine. The first issue of the revived student newspaper came out last week—just a Xeroxed newsletter, but the students are so proud. The top story was about Mandy and the police search for whoever hurt her. I'm not sure what to make of that because Mark wrote it. He even went to the police station to interview officers. If he were the guilty party, wouldn't he want to stay as far away from the police as he could? Or is he trying to hide in plain sight? We did read "The Purloined Letter" for class. He wrote a very good essay about how our brains filter things out that they think aren't important. Smart kid. Too smart?

To answer your question, I'm not sure how things are with Jon. We've been doing stuff together, and he's working to "to keep me safe." But I need my space! That's not easy with him living right above me, where he can see when I come and go. I'm afraid I'm becoming paranoid and that will hurt our relationship. We got into a fight after he had been in my apartment to install a deadbolt in the door. I thought some things were out of place and accused him of going through my things. I probably just forgot where I put stuff—I haven't been sleeping well since Mandy's death.

We haven't broken up, but things are tense. I want this to work; I need a friend here. There really is no one else I could hang out with here. I do not fit in! Not to mention that it would make living here and work awkward at best. I should probably just chill, right?

XO

MJ

Feb. 10

Dear Prof. Johns,

I need advice on how to handle my senior English class. We started discussing Updike's "The A & P" in class today. I don't know why I thought it would work to discuss a story about a teenaged boy and his reaction to three teen girls going to the grocery store in their swimsuits. I guess I thought they would relate to it. Relate they did. I was a little late getting to class (after lunch) and someone had drawn two ice cream cones on the white board with the caption "I want to lick 'the two smoothest scoops of vanilla'" under it, quoting that line from the story referring to Queenie's breasts. I tried to stick with my lesson about the story's plot, but the kids kept snickering. When I asked them to identify the story's "climax," some of the kids laughed so hard they fell out of their seats. It shouldn't have been that funny to them. I mean, I was using ASL, so I signed climax as "peak," not the other meaning—but I made the mistake of writing the word on the whiteboard, too. This one kid, Mark, told everyone to calm down and give me my C-L-I-M-A-X.

Rookie blunder? How do I salvage this and regain control of the class? Thank you in advance for any advice!

Mary Jane Bradford

Feb. 12

Jill—

Just a quick note to let you know that it looks like I was right about Mark. The cops arrested him today—not for killing Mandy, but for child porn. Apparently he hid a camera in the girls' dorm here and had videoed girls taking showers and so on. They haven't found anything connecting him to me or Mandy's death yet, but a lot of his files are encrypted. I'm sick, but relieved.

M.J.

Feb. 14

Mom,

Happy Valentine's Day! I hope you are having a good one. I wanted to tell you I love you a bunch!

Jon made me dinner tonight to celebrate Mark's arrest and Valentine's Day. Isn't that romantic?

Love,

Mary Jane

Mom and Jill—texting for safety. Turned Wifi off on my phone. I feel like I'm losing my mind. I really wish you were here with me. Both of you. Just sent you an email, Mom. Please reply as if all is OK. I'm afraid Jon is monitoring what I do on his network, and has surveillance set up in my apartment and can watch what I do there. I'm in my bed now, with the covers over my head.

I went up to Jon's for dinner. I dressed up for the occasion in high heels, a pencil skirt, and a low-cut top. He had a box of chocolate cordials for me, a little something for Valentine's Day, he said. So of course I let him kiss me. Mom, sorry you have to hear this, but he reached down and brushed my breasts, first with his hands, then with his mouth. He smiled and signed, "smoothest scoops of ice cream." He stepped back a bit and winked. I think my heart skipped a few beats. That line's from a story I just taught. How could that be random? At best, Jon's a snoop. At worst—well, I don't think I need to spell that out for you.

I couldn't think of a good way to leave right then, since we hadn't eaten dinner yet. Not that I had any appetite. I just picked at my food for a while. Then I told Jon that I wasn't feeling that well and wanted to go back to my place to lie down.

I stopped in my bathroom to splash water on my face. It wasn't exactly a lie that I don't feel good. So, I'm standing there drying my face off with the hand towel and I happened to look at the light switch plate. It's got a decorative design of flowers around the switch. Well, this time I noticed that middle of one of the flowers—a black-eyed susan—was actually just a hole. Perfect for a hidden camera—pointed straight at the shower.

My first thought was Mark, but how would he have gotten in? My second thought was Jon. My gut says he's watching my every move here. I'm afraid what he would do if he knew I thought he might be Mandy's killer—or worse. Right now, he thinks I think it is Mark. Heck, the police think it is Mark. Maybe it is. Either way, I texted the lead detective working my case, and he's on his way.

There's someone at the door.

Feb. 16

Dear Mom and Jill,

The police arrested Jon. You won't believe this. Apparently Mark had cameras all over the community—at school, but also in other places, including one in a tree outside of Jon's house. That camera caught Jon killing Mandy. Mark's lawyer negotiated a plea bargain—Mark gave them the footage in exchange for a juvenile sentence. And even though Mark has all kinds of inappropriate videos and pictures, he never shared them with anyone.

The cops even brought Mark to Jon's house so he could help them figure out Jon's computer and surveillance equipment. Jon had cameras in every room of my apartment! The school has an empty dorm staff apartment. It is tiny, but I'm moving there for now. I'm not sure I want to stay here after school is over, but I feel like I owe my students to at least finish out the year.

MJ

THURISAZ

BRIGHID MEREDITH

Greg snapped on his respirator. Razor wire and tank traps blocked the road. A faded red warning sign read: *High Frequency Hagalaz Area.* He glanced in the mirror. Mara, their eldest daughter, was reading a pulp romance. When they rolled to a stop, she looked out her window and asked, "This it?"

Greg's wife, Jan, turned in her seat to face their eldest daughter. "Proper English, please. You should have said, 'Is this it?'"

Greg rolled his eyes as he handed the map to Jan. "I need you to navigate. GPS won't work here since the Feds blocked the whole valley off the system."

"Cool!" Mara pushed her nose against the lead windows. "Looks dangerous—"

"English! And what it looks like is a waste of time." Jan opened up her sat-phone and started checking their bank accounts. "And this is a huge a waste of money—we can barely afford gas, and so help me god if you scratch the PEV!"

The Protective Environment Vehicle, or PEV, had been

a joint purchase. Both Greg and Jan had dipped deep into their savings to buy the newest model. It was even rated for fifteen minutes of sustained exposure. Family outings were supposed to have drawn the family closer together, but since they had gotten the PEV, Jan and Greg had done nothing but fight.

"Well, we can't spend the rest of our lives in a shelter. The Feds' rations will only last another half a year"—Greg tried getting Jan's attention as he spoke, but Jan kept scrolling through her phone—"and then everyone will starve, regardless of status." Greg snarled and exited the PEV. "Not that you care, since you won't look up from your goddamn phone!"

Roger, the family Doberman, barely followed Greg out before he slammed the door shut behind him. He took a minute to stretch and take a few deep breaths through his respirator. Greg reminded himself not to blame Jan—the Shattering had been hard for everyone.

The Shattering had been a series of earthquakes that devastated almost all the great cities. But the earthquakes had only been the start. The Shattering had also opened vents deep within the Earth that spewed forth Hagalaz, a poisonous corrosive gas that lingered on the planet's surface.

The valley that Greg had brought his family to bore evidence of Hagalaz. It was flat and utterly barren. Brown slime covered the ground everywhere, and the only break in the horizon was a single tabletop hill. The hill was where he was taking his family.

He cut and dragged the razor wire off the road and checked to see if there was a tank-trap: trenches and mounds of piled earth were meant to stop most vehicles from passing through. The Feds had dug them to keep citizens from entering the more dangerous Hagalaz areas. But that was before the first of the food riots, back when there were still enough soldiers left to police sites such as these.

It turned out that there had once been such a trap blocking the road, but after several years of exposure to Hagalaz, all that was left of the trench was a shallow ditch. Roger pissed on the warning sign. Greg kept his back to the PEV, unsealed his haz-suit, and did the same—pissed on the Feds' damn sign. The government didn't want people to know about the hilltop—but Greg knew all about the Feds' lies.

When Greg got back, Jan still hadn't touched the map. Instead of fighting with her, he decided to drive forward without navigation. Everything was flat anyways, and he could clearly see the hill. So he eased off the brakes, stepped on the gas, and passed into the valley. The PEV jolted as he crossed the old tank-trap, and everyone inside was jostled. Jan had been just about to open her mouth, likely to yell at Greg for possibly scratching the PEV, when a cry came from the backseat.

"Mom." Mara plugged her ears. "Tara's hungry!" Tara was the youngest in the family, still a baby, and she had just woken up from her nap.

Jan handed back a jar of baby food and told Mara to feed her younger sister. After the customary complaint, Mara obliged and began spooning the gruel into Tara's mouth. Seconds later, the cry was replaced with a happy coo.

While they drove, they saw a man walking toward the hill. The man's haz-suit was tattered at the hems, with large rips exposing his face and arms. Oozing blisters covered his bared skin. The sight of him shocked the family, and Jan locked all the doors. As they rolled past the man, he held out his hand for help, but Greg looked straight ahead and never stopped.

"Mom. Mom!" Mara had pasted herself to the back window so that she could keep watching the man. "Do you see him?!"

"Fourth-Class scum," Jan whispered under her breath. "Mara's too young to understand. This is your fault." Jan glared at Greg before turning back toward Mara. "Don't mind that man, honey. He was probably kicked out of the shelter for thieving."

They continued riding in silence.

Atop the hill were two black obelisks standing a meter apart. The Feds had denied they existed, but Greg had discovered them in an old podcast. The two obelisks together formed a thurisaz, or a gateway. A person who walked through a thurisaz would disappear and would theoretically re-emerge in a land without Hagalaz. But since no one had ever returned, the theory was still unconfirmed.

Greg left his family in the PEV at the base of the hill while he scouted ahead. He walked around the thurisaz, running a hand across the black stone. Despite the distance, he thought he could hear Tara crying again. He glanced down the hill, back toward the PEV, and saw the smoke. The smoke blanketed the land in the distance—it was mostly white, with tints of yellow. There was no mistaking it: Hagalaz.

He heard slime slurping under someone's footstep, and thought that Jan had sent Mara up to get him. He turned, with the words already on his lips, "I told you to wait—" But it wasn't Mara. The man that they had driven past on the valley floor, the man in the tattered Hazmat suit, had reached the top of the hill. Greg backed away, wishing he had a weapon. But the man never so much as glanced at Greg; he just looked up to heaven, stretched his arms out, smiled wide enough for a blister on his lip to split open, and stumbled through the thurisaz. He then disappeared completely.

Greg circled the gateway. No trace was left of the man. Again, Greg felt the columns—smooth, cold, and now humming slightly. Holding his breath, he thrust his arm through the gateway—but nothing happened. He thought that it only would work if a person stepped completely through. He was tempted to walk through it then and there, but the temptation was momentary. He refused to leave without his family, including Roger.

The wind shifted, and Hagalaz started rolling toward the hill. Greg ran back toward the PEV, cutting corners, leaping over the stray boulder. He slipped and landed in the brown sludge, getting the slime all over his backside. He had to stop a moment to check his suit—it was stained, and would stink. But it had no penetrations, so it was still functional.

He found his family waiting below. The PEV's recirculators were running, and Mara had been watching a show on one of the PEV's monitors. Greg opened the door, still panting from his run down the hill. "It's up there. The thurisaz, it's actually up there!"

Jan showed him her phone. "A report said Hagalaz is headed our way." A blinking red hazard light was flashing over an image of the hilltop. "We need to leave."

"We still have time." Greg tried explaining, but Roger jumped up on him and slobbered all over his facemask. Roger's tail was wagging vigorously, and kept hitting Mara in the face.

"Dad!" Mara complained as she tried pushing Roger's tail away.

"No." Jan pointed out the window. The setting sun fell behind the hill and threw a shadow over the PEV while painting the distant Hagalaz red. "We need to leave now. Besides, the Feds think the thurisaz and Hagalaz are related—"

"Jan, I saw that man go through. You have got to believe me ... He just disappeared."

"He's probably dead then." Jan crossed her arms. "Well? You saw your stupid thurisaz. And we paid a fortune to drive you here, but now that you've seen it, can we please go?!"

"Go where? Back to the shelter? To starve? Food's running out." Greg grabbed the keys and got out.

"It's only temporary!" Jan shouted. "The Feds are making new warrens, with hydroponics—"

"Everyone out!" Greg opened the back door. Roger jumped out, tail and ears flat. Roger wore protective boots over his paws to protect against any residual acid on the ground. The boots wouldn't provide full-body protection to Roger though. If Hagalaz hit, then Roger wouldn't last more than thirty seconds. But Hagalaz wouldn't hit, at least not before Greg got Roger and the rest of the family through the thurisaz. After that, haz-suits wouldn't matter. Everyone would be safe.

Mara groaned but finally got out. Greg unbuckled Tara from her baby-seat and carried her on his shoulders.

When Mara was out of earshot, Jan hissed: "You are killing us."

Greg was the last up the hill. He had carried Tara the whole way up. Hagalaz had just enveloped the hill's base, making the hilltop an island in a sea of sulfuric poison. Down below, Hagalaz covered the land, including the PEV.

When the fog rolled over the PEV, Jan swore, "What a waste of a fucking fortune." She spoke loudly enough for the kids to hear this time, her English as immaculate as ever, despite the profanity. But Jan's angry voice still upset Tara, and Greg had to bounce the baby to keep her from crying.

"We aren't going to need it where we're going," Greg

reminded her. They had reached the top and they stopped to stare at the obelisks. The black stones rose ten meters into the air, making an impressive monument. Even more impressive was the fact that the glyphs etched across the stone remained clear and legible.

Jan thumbed toward the obelisks. "This is it? You wasted everything just to see this?!"

"They aren't a pile of sludge yet, are they?" Greg said. Unlike all the rest of the world, the obelisks seemed immune to Hagalaz. Even iron and steel would succumb to Hagalaz, but these black rocks were made of something else entirely, possibly otherworldly.

While Jan and Greg argued, Mara circled the glyphs and began tracing them out with her delicate and perfect fingers. After going around the thurisaz once, she turned to Greg with a huge smile on her face. "They vibrate!"

"—stay away from those!" Jan yelled from a distance. She refused to get anywhere close to the thurisaz. "Those *rocks* are dangerous!"

"Not as dangerous as that." Greg pointed. The wind continued blowing against the hill which caused the Hagalaz to climb. Down below the PEV's alarm went off—the five-minute warning, five minutes until the last of the PEV's plastic shielding dissolved. Jan almost started back down the hill as though to save the PEV.

"Jan!" Greg blocked her path. "You won't make it. It's too far. Besides, we don't need it!"

Jan swore again. She turned to the thurisaz. "How do your precious"—she waved her hands at the obelisks—"work then?" She stepped closer to it, stopping right in front of a caution sign, a placard glued to an obelisk.

"We just walk through." Greg handed Tara to Jan and took a step—his foot just crossed the threshold—

"Wait!" Jan said. "Send the dog first ..."

The fog was rising, but it wasn't even halfway up the hill yet. There was still time to humor Jan, if it would get her to cross the threshold with Greg.

Jan took hold of Roger's collar as Greg walked around the obelisks. He got down on his knees, careful not to scratch his suit on the gravel. "Roger, come boy!"

Jan let Roger go, but instead of running through the gate as Greg had intended, the Doberman ran completely around and jumped onto Greg, licking his facemask.

"No, through the gate, go through it!" Greg tried forcing the dog through, but the dog's claws scraped against the ground. "Get through it!" Greg grabbed Roger's collar and tail and heaved.

Roger growled. Greg swore and he pushed harder. Roger turned and snapped at Greg, his jaws clamped around the edge of Greg's sleeve just as he was jumping back. Dog and man eyed each other for seconds, until finally Greg gave up and stepped back.

"See?" Jan said. "Even your dog knows! The gates are suicide."

"That man went through—"

"We're stranded, the PEV's destroyed, and, and—God damnit to fucking hell!" Jan put Tara under one arm and pulled out her phone.

"Jan, just give it a try. You haven't even tried—"

"They are just fucking rocks!" Jan slammed a number into the phone. Her phone clicked—"Second Class, code 10211—send a fucking evac!" She glared at the fog rising, and then she yelled: "Mara, get over here!"

Only silence answered.

"Mara!?" Jan called again. Worry tainted her voice.

A voice crackled on the phone, "Geolocations received. Extraction en-route."

Greg sprinted the hill's circumference, checking all the sides, even the way they had come. But by now, the Hagalaz was lapping at the top of the hill, like gentle waves upon a shore. He couldn't see through the fog, and he was forced to step back as a few wisps of Hagalaz flowed onto the hilltop.

Greg flipped on his suit's amplifier: "Mara!" He screamed as he ran another circuit around. She couldn't be down there—she would never be that stupid. But she didn't answer ... Then he realized that Mara must have already gone through the thurisaz.

"Hurry!" Jan screamed into the phone. She stepped away from the Hagalaz reaching toward her.

"She went through the gate!" Greg shouted as he came back. The Hagalaz had almost reached the thurisaz. "We need to go through, now!"

"She's dead—you killed her!" Jan screamed, her mascara running down her face. Even with a faceplate, she was still pretty, even without the layers of makeup.

Greg tried again, now desperate to convince his wife. "She's alive. Jan, there's a better world, just through those obelisks. Mara went through, and so will we."

"She's dead ... oh God—she's really dead ..."

"Give me Tara." Greg took a step toward Jan. "I'll go through first."

Jan jerked back, stepping into the fog, up to her shins. "Get away!"

A voice on the phone: "Ma'am, what's happening."

"He wants my baby to go through the gate—"

"Stay away from it! Christ, we try warning people ... The Air-Vac is almost there."

Hagalaz reached the very summit of the hill and covered the base of the thurisaz. Harsh vapors, including a potent form of sulfuric acid, pushed against everyone's haz-suits, except for Roger, who was bare and exposed. Greg ran for him. He had to get Roger through the gate! But the vapors reached Roger before Greg did. Roger's hair was singed off and his legs audibly sizzled. Hagalaz pushed against everything—Greg's PTFE pants pressed into his legs, warm from the chemical reaction beginning to eat through his haz-suit. The heat sped the reaction, producing more heat.

"Through the gate!" Greg shouted, trying to push Roger through, but the dog wouldn't listen.

Roger jumped up. His protective boots had already disintegrated. Claws raked Greg's chest. Skin flapped loose around the dog's thighs and black chunks sloughed off Roger's legs.

"Go through the gate ..." Greg whispered, thinking feebly of his plan to get Roger through the thurisaz, or back down into the PEV if the gate did not work. But the PEV was already dissolved by the acid.

The dog's eyes dissolved into a gel. A white froth covered his muzzle and chest. His tail had completely disappeared. Roger—Greg's eight-year-old Doberman, from before the Shattering, possibly one of the last Dobermans left on the continent, with whom Greg had shared his own rations, even when the Feds had started cutting down—gave one last shudder, a piteous whine, and he fell back, sliding off from Greg's chest and down into the rising Hagalaz.

"Give me Tara!" Greg screamed.

"Stay back!" Jan stepped further into the fog, holding Tara above her head.

Tara reached for Greg, a pudgy gloved hand outstretched. "Dada?"

A helicopter approached. They heard it first: *thu-thu-THU-THUWACK.* Then they saw the orange helicopter flying toward them. The turbulence from its blades stirred the fog below. Jan screamed and waved Tara over her head. "HERE!"

Hagalaz reached chest height. Searing tendrils snaked across Greg's chest. He smelled rotten eggs and screamed as he realized his suit was leaking. Roger must have ruined his suit! Greg fumbled to find the damage, and found shreds along the front. In vain, he groped for his Teflon tape, even though he knew that he could never repair the damage quickly enough. He gasped. His tongue burned—his nose—*Oh, God*—his eyes! Hagalaz enveloped him. His mask fogged. Pressure. Darkness. He keeled, hit the ground, but the pressure only worsened. Acid spread, following the seams inside his suit. Each second became agony, and he prayed for death.

Jan was screaming, and something shook his shoulders. He turned over and by some miracle saw the obelisks looming over him. To his right he found Roger's skeleton, already crumbling apart. In an effort of great will, Greg rose to his feet. Every joint and sinew screamed, and his chest tightened until he thought his heart would explode. He couldn't breathe. One of the rescuers hung down from a ladder nearby, reaching for him. Jan and Tara were already in the helicopter. The man grabbed Greg's shoulders, and Greg almost let himself be rescued. But the thurisaz was only a step away. Greg yanked free and tumbled through the gateway.

When he opened his eyes, he was under a sky filled with odd stars. The softest grass tickled his cheeks. As he sat up, he found that his haz-suit was gone, along with the rest of his clothes. His skin was pink and fleshy and unscarred. The thurisaz was behind him, and in front of him was a great river of the purest water he'd ever seen. And on the other side of the river, waving for him to follow, was his daughter Mara.

IN THE HAUNTED DARKNESS

MICHAEL R. COLLINGS

I am not mad.

Note how calmly I can make that declaration. Listen to the evenness in my voice, the smoothness of my blood flowing through my veins as I repeat it:

I am not mad.

I know ... I know. Others have made the same declamation, only to have their protests proved false by their ghastly aberrancies.

But I ... *I* know ... I *know* that the sounds I hear are safely locked within the thin-walled cabinet of my skull, that they cannot take on a frightful life, a horrifying tangibility. They are nothing more than the constant firing of nerve cells linking half-deaf ears to brain, a sea-storm of waving cilia.

And I know that there is nothing medicine can do to forestall the constant barrage of sounds.

To some degree, I have learned to live with my condition.

Right.

Severe deafness is bad enough.

Living with tinnitus is Hell.

Days are really not so difficult. I have private means, so I needn't contend face-to-face with the mindless hordes of fast-tongued, slurring consumers who would make communicating unbearable. Nor do I have to listen to the endless riffle of pages turning as I make meaningless computations on a softly sputtering computer screen. I can seek out environments that generate sufficient noise that I don't notice my internal cacophony ... almost.

My time is my own.

I can take long walks. The wind—however slight, there seems *always* to be a breeze near where I live—fluttering against my ear-porches nearly masks the underlying crackles, sizzles, and staticky wheezes. Even the sounds of my heels on concrete walkways or asphalt pavements can help...and for that reason I wear distinctive high-heeled boots with arced steel taps affixed. *Tap-tap-tap swisssssssh tap-tap-tap.*

And there are other options.

I spend long afternoons at a nearby fast-food joint, relishing dollar-a-cup refillable drinks and cheap food. I needn't pay close attention to what anyone there says. I do not know them—indeed, I carefully refrain from cultivating even an all-too-casual *howdy-de-do* level of acquaintance. I do not know them. They do not know me, except perhaps as the frequent purchaser of a certain sandwich and an all-you-can-drink soda from their limited menu.

The bridge over the river sometimes invites me. There is a concrete railing just chest-high where I can rest my arms and lean over the balustrade to watch the infinitely changeable currents of light and shadow on the surface and listen to the subtle *hiss-gurgle-slap* as water swirls around the weathered marble pillars ... at almost the same volume as my sounds. Almost.

And there are other distractions.

Colors. Shapes. Surfaces glinting and angling and casting eldritch shadows even at the height of noon.

So.

Days are not too difficult.

But nights. Ah, nights. The times of incipient madness, when it seems as if my head must burst and all the captured noise spill like clotted blood to spatter against walls and floor and ceiling. When it seems that I might lay on one side, ear flattened against the thin mattress—even though that accentuates rather than muffles the sounds. I close my eyes so tightly that tears start almost against my will; and half-pretend half-pray that my ear is but a conduit to some vast underground vault, lined with time-effaced bricks and fouled with the cast-off hopes and fears of negligent humanity, and that my sounds will trickle from my brain, through the ear, and dissipate among the noisome jetsam.

Darkness and loneliness and silence and despair press around me.

Those are the difficult times.

Tinnitus is Hell.

Or rather, those *were* the difficult times.

Because of late, I have made a rather startling discovery, one which even now I can barely comprehend.

It began on an otherwise nondescript night. The sounds were neither more intrusive nor less than usual. Indeed, I had almost grown used to them as they winnowed their way through the darkness with the treadless stealth of ghosts.

I recall that I had taken up another of my strategies for dealing with them ... cataloging them, screwing my eyelids tight against the blackness, and constructing a mind-chart that would tell me where ... and what ... each sound might be.

The closest ones came first.

The *hmmmmm-buzz-static* just beneath the surface of my left ear. On my mind-chart, it would be represented by a fine red line, perhaps only half an inch long, midway between the pinna and the eardrum. It might, perhaps, vibrate slightly, just beneath the terminus of sight.

Almost touching the outer flesh of my left ear, the *clatter-rattle-click* of a dozen nuts and bolts being shaken violently in a fragile glass jar.

Then the electrical *crackle* that formed a tight sphere not more than nine inches from my left ear, hovering in the silent air, taking up a slightly more dorsal position than ventral.

Next, the frenetic *tic-tic-tic*, as of a hyperactive alarm clock nestled just where my neck met the pillowcase, a *tic-tic-tic-tic* so rapid that I felt my heartbeat hasten to make up for lost time.

I did not have an alarm clock in my bedroom. Even though I occasionally hear one ring, I do not own an alarm clock.

Somewhere a door closed with a muffled *thump*. Footsteps echoed on the carpeted stairway leading to my bedroom. From the doorway, someone whispered my name. Once.

I was alone in my house. I am always alone.

These sounds—and more—were part of my every moment. They were the standard of routine.

I finished my normal catalogue of the bangs, clatters, and rattles that surround my head like some insane diving helmet composed of fractured sound rather than clear, pure, crystalline glass. Then, for reasons I still do not comprehend,

I reached outward, beyond the protective borders of my house.

First I found the sound of shovels—broad lips of sharpened steel grating against the concrete sidewalks, scraping away non-existent snow half-melting in the one-hundred-plus degree August night-time heat. *Scrape. Scrape. Scrape.* As rhythmical as if I were observing some night watchman laboring at his task, struggling to remove the snowfall faster than it accumulated. *Scrape. Scrape. Scrape.*

(All of this time, of course, the nearer sounds continued unabated, if anything sharpened by my attention to sounds outside my window.)

Somewhere down the street, the whine of an electric garage-door opener. Up. Down. Up. Down. *Whine-roar.*

Just beyond the garage door, a motorcycle wailed into the night. Once. Twice. Three times, each time softer than the last until it disappeared. Almost.

Further yet, the muffled bellow of eighteen-wheeler caravans on the ten-mile-distant freeway, low and warm, smelling of exhausted ozone and overheated rubber tires. Almost—*almost*—could I hear the individual music of each tire, the *hummm* of each separate tread.

Usually, this was as far as I would go. On a good night, I would be asleep by this time. On a bad night, the susurration of the faraway traffic—not discernable by ears used only to more mundane sounds—would eventually lull me into dreams. Vivid dreams. Long, frantic dreams that would make me yearn to wake.

But tonight, for the first time, I ventured even—ever—further outward, beyond the flat and uninspiring landscapes of this Earth and into the vast regions of the unending space that surrounds this petty point of life.

I approached Jupiter, Bringer of Jollity. How I longed—

yearned—to slow and refresh myself in the not-quite subliminal chaos of its storms, its gigantic eye peering up at me as I listened, unblinking, reassuring.

Then, with the nearly infinite speed of human thought, I passed beyond the orbit of Saturn, Bringer of Old Age, and felt myself bend beneath the weight of uncounted—uncountable—centuries. I would have paused, listened to the friction-*hiss* of its jeweled rings, but already my frenzied course had increased, catapulting me into the lifeless depths beyond.

But my speed allowed only for the briefest hint of something like music, something like static, something like the labored breathing of a monstrous beast before I was whisked beyond, arcing into frozen night with such rapidity that I felt I must soon reach the awesome maw of the great Black Hole that surely lies at the heart of this galaxy. Mentally I closed my eyes—they were open where my body lay, not yet asleep on the thin, lumpy mattress in my bedroom—and strained to feel ... to *feel*, not *see*, limitless space as it flashed by.

If I had been travelling in a physical body at even an infinitesimal fraction of the speed I had attained, I would have been instantaneously crushed, if not utterly discorporated. Abruptly, I encountered a barrier at once definitely solid and yet so diaphanous that I could almost hear the remote stars whispering, "*Come, come, come.*" But I could not.

Instead, I began to *hear* colors, some familiar—viridian, cardinal, cobalt, xanthous—others such as the human eye has never seen, furious whirling and wheeling of light-not-darkness, of hues beyond description and recall; yet each, even those few for which I could find a name, seemed touched by something wild, something untamed and untamable, something ineffably dark and ... dare I say it ... *evil.*

Something *eldritch.*

Within the color-sounds and the sound-colors, I detected yet something more, something that seemed to come from behind me. A voice perhaps, or many speaking in the choral unison of legions, speaking in a language I did not, *could not* know, and still I understood: "*Come back. What you seek awaits you on your own petty world, not in the regions of distant space. Your resolution—my Restoration—awaits here. Come back ...*"

And a force as of huge tentacles, fibrous, muscular, irresistible and enormous, pulled against me, became tangible against my nothing-flesh, grasped harder with a deadly cold, and began to penetrate toward the center of my warmth and being.

It was a threat.

Return or die.

I heard the aggregation of millennia of miles unwind as I slipped backwards, through the spheres of Saturn, of Jupiter, and of Mars, and finally through the sphere of the Moon itself, careening backward into sublunar space until abruptly I hovered—*hearing* only, mind you, not seeing or feeling, bereft even of the sense of those cyclopean tentacles that had wrapped around my being—just above the surface of the ocean's deepest abyss.

For an instant that lasted longer than my lifetime of memories, I heard only the almost soothing murmur of ocean waves as they roiled ceaselessly above unfathomable depths. They soothed, they smoothed, they smothered all sounds but themselves.

Then: "*Welcome.*"

I could hear the colossal size of its speaker, its frigid antiquity beyond all human history, beyond all human cares, its coldness, its utter *alienness*—these manifested themselves in the timbre of the sound, in the unbreathing, inorganic difference from anything I had ever heard before. I heard the meanings, not the words muttered in some pre-pre-Adamic language never meant to be articulated by a human tongue.

"Come closer."

Beneath me, I heard the whispering waves draw nearer, close around me, and I sank deeper and deeper into the abyss until I heard something more: the wash of currents around monolithic stones, the *hiss* of Stygian dwellers directed even toward the phantom of an interloper.

"Come to me, o nugatory one, and I—even I the Chief of All—will give you what you wish for."

"What I ...?"

"What you wish for more than anything in this world or in the worlds beyond. I will give you this one great thing. All that you must do is to return once more, to the surface, and speak the words I will give you, words that will open the gateway between your world and mine. A simple thing ... a choice, really. Refuse to speak, and you will live ... and suffer ... forever. Or open the gate, and die ... along with all the Earth. But you *will know quietude."*

"But ..."

"Speak the words. Only then I will grant you ...

"Serenity ...

"Stillness ...

"Siiiiiiilencccccce ..."

While the final sibilants insinuated themselves into my mind, I fell into dream: a dream of a hidden megalopolis, its tremendous stones resting, sleeping, waiting beneath the waves, its massive structures, its tortuous thoroughfares of great stone ramps, its behemoth citadels that dwarfed all mortal trials in petty grandeur and foolish grandiosity. For endless hours—in the dream—I wandered through broad avenues, with bas-reliefs incised into the living stone, with statues standing free at intersections, with murals on every surface … all depicting such wondrous horrors, such loathly terrors that they cannot be named … we mortals have not the words, have not the *consciousness* of the words, would not dare speak the words if they existed.

Yet I suddenly knew certain words, a litany of rhythmic utterance beyond all meaning and beyond all hope that would open an imprisoning gateway and recall the mighty city to the surface. Awaken the sleeping god—*behemoth, leviathan, kraken, Cthulhu,* by whatever outré name known—and restore the Outer Ones to their ancient place within the universe. Condemn humanity to be toyed with, to their suffering agonies of slavery, torture, and eventual, inevitable death.

And all the time I knew it was a *dream*, just as I had known my voyages through space, the voices and the words I heard there were *not*, because there were no sounds except the touch of water on time-polished stone. No *clack-hiss-buzz-pop-screech.*

In my dreams, I *never* hear the sounds. Only when I awaken do they return to launch once again their insistent attack.

In that monstrous city, there were no sounds. Blessedly, no sounds.

I could choose silence … and death. Or live forever with that which pounds inside my head. Neither a blessing; both a curse.

Living is Choice.

Choice is Hell.

I awoke when the sun first broke over the distant mountain crests and shattered through my window. Immediately—

more rapidly than *immediately*—the sounds resumed. Immediately I struggled to ignore them.

I went at once to my computer and began to write, to record what I had heard, as best I could.

I know that I cannot continue as I have, slave and subject to the random firings of nerves, interpreted by my brain as sounds.

In my bathroom cabinet are the bottles of pills my doctors have prescribed to help me sleep. There are enough, I think, to bring me what I most devoutly wish. Provided that what I experienced was a dream, and that I am not cursed to live forever, should I fail to make the choice expected of me.

Someone once wrote:

> By the silence
> I will know
> That I am dead.

There are enough to grant me that.

But ... what if ...?

I am not mad. I know the difference between Dream and not-Dream.

And thus ... Perhaps ... Perhaps ...

SPIRIT BOX
KRISTEN HARMON

She liked ghosts, and I liked her.

My uncle was in the business of metal detectors and Civil War junk, so when she asked about ghost soldiers, I asked her to drive around battlefields with me.

That's how it got started. At the end of the spring, just before I dropped out of college my junior year, we decided to rent an attic apartment at the top of an old white Spanish-style mansion called *Beuna Vista,* near Antietam battlefield. She had always wanted to live there in that square white house with wide, flat windows, topped with curved arches like eyebrows, and a crown on top of the house—a widow's walk. She thought she had a memory of living nearby with a kind lady she called her grandmother.

Wait, she'd told me the first time we drove up the ridge and nearly past the house. She'd seen a handwritten sign taped to a huge, round, rusting mailbox at the end of a long gravel driveway. It was the kind of sign that was always intended to be overlooked.

I eased off the gas, let the car coast to a full stop, and grinned at her when it started drifting back down the hill toward the house, on its own. I had just finished rebuilding it, a Pontiac Fiero that I'd reclaimed from my uncle's grown-over backyard, next to a rusted pile of Confederate mortar shells and a charred forest of dumped Christmas trees I'd stuck standing straight up in the ground and burned. The Fiero growled and barked under my feet every time I pressed the gas pedal and shifted gears to power up and down the mountains at the state lines, but it was bad-ass. Spray-painted a matte black. I loved it and called it my Beast. At the very last second, I braked and idled in front of the house, and the car shook and rattled its shell and bones.

Taped to the box with an old-fashioned clear yellow tape, the kind with threads, and written in blue ball-point in spindly WWII cursive, the sign said, *"Historic Mountain Resort Beuna Vista now open to quality tenants; enquire at front door."* Green tree pollen dusted the top of the spreading rust on the mailbox, the kind of rust that looks like it's peeling back to a dry red bone. It was almost pretty, and I sneezed.

Finish-seen this before, she said, looking up at the house. She looked down at her hand and spelled out the name of the house as if she'd read it somewhere a long time ago and was trying to remember. *B-e-u-n-a V-i-s-t-a,* she repeated, a frown on her face. *It's misspelled. Supposed to be Beautiful View. In Spanish.*

Isn't the view supposed to be what *the house* sees? This was the actual view: the slopes and squares of the farms and yellow and black squares of the national park below us.

[SIC], she told me, with a smile.

I smiled back, thinking I understood, but puzzled as to why she didn't use the sign that meant touched-in-the-head.

Not sick, she explained with both air brackets and air quotes. S-*u-c-h a-s i-t w-a-s. Means original contained a mistake.*

That's how it was written. No corrections. Left as is.

Who couldn't love a girl who knew how to add in air brackets? She always liked to explain things to me; I was the college student, and she wasn't. She'd graduated from the deaf school two years after me, and she worked at the used book and DVD warehouse.

Now means Screwed-up View?

You're sick. She laughed.

S-i, s-i, I'd told her, with a two-handed bowing down.

Latin, silly, she'd said. But she'd laughed.

I still remember what she looked like at that moment, the spring sun on her face, the chilly wind blowing in from the open windows. It's always sunny and cold, in my mind, when I think about her outside that house.

It turned out that Beuna Vista had only two owners since it was built in the 1920s, and the Earnshays, an elderly hearing couple were the second ones. They didn't know who had named the house or why, except it used to be a sanitarium for TB patients. While Stella stood outside on the house's patio and wrote back and forth with the Earnshays, I waited outside, leaned back against the Beast, and tilted my face up to the bleary spring sun.

Echoing me, Stella leaned back on the peeling black wrought iron rail, and I caught myself worrying that it would give way and she would fall off the patio. I could almost see it happening, and for a moment it was like it already did happen but then that moment folded in on itself and was gone. Falling in love like this felt like a trippy fever coming on, but I'd take it.

The stucco on the outside walls on the first floor had been painted recently, the pox scars of a bad plaster job bubbling up and flaking here and there. I wanted to get a black Sharpie and circle those crusted bumps because I swear they moved, but maybe it's just the shadows from the studded branches of the nearby trees or it's that same broken blood vessel floating by on the wall behind my eyes.

She walked back to me and my matte-black behemoth, a huge smile on her face. *It's perfect,* she said. *Looks like a barge—big, wide, slow.* And it did look like a white boat on top of that grassy mound.

So that, she told me, was the first thing you have to do if you're going to try to recover lost memories like we did for her that summer; you have to get an appropriately becalmed apartment. She'd been reading about spirits, shamans, and mediums in the back room of the book warehouse. Recovering lost memories seemed to her like resurrecting dead people; if you could recover a memory, then there also would be the person. She believed that all will reveal itself, if you let it.

I feel LaLa is nearby, she said to me before we drove away. *She's waiting.*

She'd gotten into the whole repressed memory thing through her boyfriend Nix, one of those guys who everyone liked but there was something off about him. For me, it was the way that he watched people watching him tell a joke or a story. There was something blank behind his face—that's the best way I can describe it.

Of course, we didn't tell anyone what we were doing. It sounded crazy. It was crazy. At least my cover story of setting up some kind of themed tie-in with my uncle's junkyard was socially acceptable. And I really had always wanted to set up a battlefield ghost tour; that was never a lie.

After the Earnshays got over the fact that we were both deaf, that we had drivers' licenses, and that I was still at that time a college student, our new landlords kept their views to themselves. We knew that the religious Earnshays gave us the side-eye, an unmarried college-age guy and a girl living together in the darkest, warmest part of the house.

I didn't want to ask my parents for the deposit money, so I sold my cranky beast of a car for almost nothing. God, walking off the Mason-Dixon Used Car lot felt like I'd left my balls behind. It almost felt like the car, now parked under an old cat-eye lamppost, watched me go.

Sometimes I wonder what would have happened differently if I'd kept my metal babe, my matte-black chariot, and worked at the liquor store instead for the cash money. But then that would have meant that I'd be away from her more often. It would have been the same thing at the end.

After our deposit cleared and we moved in on the first hot day in May, the Earnshays left us a chatty, relieved-sounding note to say that they were related to the Earnshaws of *Wuthering Heights*—even though the Earnshaws were made up—and anyway, a "w" was not the same as a "y." *W is the new Y,* I told Stella. *Just call me R-A-W.* She always smiled when I said that. *You're funny,* she'd say. And that was everything.

I made a lot of fun of the Earnshays to Stella, but that gave her the idea to re-read the novel that summer, and she did, curled up in the window seat of the widow's walk in the one cool, rainy week in June. It's probably still there, right where she left it. We seem to have been the last and only tenants the Earnshays took in. They never did anything with the house except the clipping and cutting back of the landscaping and other stuff on the outside. As far as I know, they left everything inside as it was when we lived there—and before us, just as the first owners had left it.

Most afternoons at 1:15 p.m., Mrs. Earnshay walked around outside in huge wrap-around black shades and a blue denim work shirt, the sleeves always buttoned at the wrist, no matter how hot or chilly the day. One day, an especially bright and windy day, she wore a fleece hunting balaclava mask with her wrap-around shades. When I saw her, it took me so long to figure out who or what she was, my heart pounded, and I felt like I was lost. Mrs. Earnshay looked like something too carefully inhabiting those shabby clothes, an imposter with a round head and flat bug eyes.

Mrs. Earnshay's daily constitutional seemed to consist of not much more than checking each of the tiny, aging, boutique trees in the front, pausing, but not touching, each set of knotted branches, dying back one by one like strange hands on the lawn.

They had no visitors even though they went to a church down in the valley and there was a sepia-toned picture of two small children in vintage hats and coats, a boy and a girl, on a round wooden table in their hallway. We only saw the inside of the main house once, when we gave them the check, and after that, we took the freshly-cut, still green, wooden stairs up to our door in the widow's walk. The one window that we could see from the stairs was always shuttered and dark. Of course that also meant they could never see who was on the stairs up to the widow's walk apartment.

I saw in the paper Mrs. Earnshay died this past fall, releasing her skin promptly at 1:15 p.m. The obituary mentioned that the house's original owners, Adrien and Lara Cuvelier, had originally built the house to be shared with her family, but their boat sank on the crossing over the Atlantic. After Lara died of influenza in the house, Mr. Cuvelier allowed it to be used as a sanitarium for WWII patients until the Earnshays, a young couple with two children, bought the place. Mrs. Earnshay had been a nurse stationed in this sanitarium.

The Earnshays probably didn't know how easy they had it with us as tenants. We kept mostly to ourselves. Stella quit her job, and we stayed up most of the night, slept through most of the day. But the mail was obviously sifted through before being neatly stacked just outside the apartment door, each bill facing upwards, the addresses all to the right. I'd left college and hadn't yet paid off the balance from the previous semester, so my mail had a tendency to pile up.

We spent those days and nights together in what now feels to me like a warm, sleepy haze, the hot late afternoon sun streaming in through the windows, the spiky pattern of the succulents—Stella's plants—moving slowly across the room.

The attic—I haven't yet described what it looked like inside—was what you'd expect of an old attic. Gouged wooden floors, old bedsteads—now gone—having screeched and scratched across the splintering boards. One bed: a fold-out full-size futon, lumpy and scratchy with cheap dollar store sheets that never got washed enough.

Stella preferred the long window-seat of the widow's walk, which opened out onto a terrace with a rail like a crown on top of the house. Lots of narrow windows up there, the wooden sills stained and rotting from rainstorms decades long gone. The breeze swept down the valley on the other side of us and up to the top of the house even on the hottest nights that summer. I bought her a porch chaise cushion to soften the old wooden seat.

I painted the sepia walls white to give it a fresh look when we first moved in. Stella scrounged up old blue and green apothecary bottles from Goodwill and used those for decorations. Some still have sprigs of Stella's flowers in them. You can see them even now in the windows.

I feel like I've been here for a-g-e-s, she'd said, with a rare, contented, smile. *It's ours.*

But there was a corner where I wouldn't look even on

the hottest, brightest nights, the full moon or the snow shining straight in. She'd just left Nix, and I took it slow that summer. I was there for her, and her alone. Together we were enough.

I'd always had a crush on Stella, with the warm brown hair and the white tank top she always wore, the one that barely covered her perfect, loveable, body. And that summer, she was there, finally, with me.

But not totally. Sometimes she startled so badly at nothing—a shadow or a touch—that I began to wonder why she didn't trust me. Wasn't I enough? After everything I'd done for her? Other times she couldn't settle down and focus. She couldn't understand why LaLa wasn't coming through the way she thought she would when we moved in.

Stella didn't have anyone; her bio parents had been druggies or transients, no one really knew. All she knew was that they had come to town in a Vega the color of mustard and stopped first at the drive-in for a foot-long hotdog and tater tots. Deafness had saved her, she said. She'd been placed in a large foster family near the school for the deaf. Her foster mom was fantastic, but she had that kind of unfocused warmth that wasn't particular to anyone. Foster mom hugged everyone the same: long, full-chested, and fresh-bread-warm.

But instead of Lala, the kind woman who she thought might have been her grandmother, Stella dreamed often of old-time soldiers marching and running below us, parting like water around the stone and mortar foundation of the house. She said she wondered if they wanted her to follow them.

Maybe this—a pathway, she told me one night, when we sat outside, dangling our feet over the edge of the walkway at the top of the house. *So they know where to go.*

At the time, I thought maybe the most important thing to do was to just let this fixation sweat itself out like a summer cold. I hadn't had that much real experience with women beyond what I taught myself with her, long and slow and short and quick, on the dollar store sheets. Seeing her close her eyes and lift herself up to me: I thought that was everything she needed.

But as June warmed up into July, she stopped chatting as much and seemed to be moving slower and slower. She perked up whenever we talked about what should be done next to get in touch with LaLa. When we planned our scouting adventures, she seemed more like herself, like the outgoing, vivacious, smiling girl I'd known as Nix's girlfriend in high school.

So if LaLa wasn't coming to us, we'd have to go to her. What we had to do next was to get something to track changes in the environment. Stella's new theory about our house was that it functioned more like an eddy in a stream, spooling down from some other spiritually active site like Antietam, but not staying still. We couldn't use the spirit boxes my uncle rigged up from Radio Shack parts and sometimes sold in his shop; spirit boxes sent out white noise and scan radio frequencies and electromagnetic fields for possible spoken responses from the ether. That was out for two deafies like us.

So I bought an EMF meter from Sears for $27.25, intended to measure electromagnetic activity. At college, I'd declared a history major, then became a sociology major, and then started an engineering major just before I'd dropped out. I didn't have a strong enough math background. But reading the manual for the EMF—all those terms: dosimeters, milligausses, field, axis, geomagnetic measurements—brought back a charge that I'd been missing. I'd been a little bored.

How your family become fascinated—dead soldiers and battlefields? she'd asked me, looking up from the EMF manual. Sweat trickled down into her beautiful cleavage. It struck me that she saw my family as holding a possible kinship for her on a metaphysical level, and maybe not on a blood and bones level, my level.

What could I say? The truth is that piles of bronze coins, minie balls, glass shards, tin tokens, and pieces of finger or foot bones didn't mean anything to me growing up. That was stuff people left behind. These were always lying around the house in muddy five-gallon buckets, waiting to be cleaned up and sold.

But ever since I was a kid in Whitford's fifth grade Western Civ. class, and I saw pictures of the crawling plaster of paris figures of Pompeii, I'd felt horrified, even angry, by the agonized absences people left behind. Living where we did, the older Deaf staff at the school told stories about soldiers walking through the night, streaming up and around the minie-ball splintered trees, gliding around the base of the house, disappearing into the woods.

Even now, sometimes, when I get up and it's a specific kind of early morning in September, still dark, smelling of leaves drying on the trees, I pause before I turn on the headlights. And then see a pair of glass eyes staring back at me. Sometimes the hands on those raccoons can look so much like small, gloved hands.

Suppose you capture soldiers, Confederates? she asked me, not seriously. *I'd ask them their names—what,* I had replied. She loved the strange spellings of the names we saw in the nation's first official cemeteries nearby. Bumpas, Corbell, Ulysses, Bushrod, even an Unthank.

What you think is my real name? she asked me.

I think—I'll name you P-r-u-d-e-n-c-e U-n-t-h-a-n-k, I told her with a grin.

Ha ha, she said and stuck her tongue out.

I walked around our attic, pointing the meter and seeing the needle pulse in response to the hidden life of the house. Stella took my other arm, and we slowly promenaded in and around each corner and across our attic. The needle seemed almost alive, like the hair on the back of your neck, but even better, engineered. The fan and the clock both pulsed the needle, just a flick, like a finger tapping.

But the needle leapt up and stayed pressed to the right when we walked closer to the bathroom. Laughing, we squeezed ourselves through the door and into the small space. I handed the meter to Stella and she held it low before her like a dowsing rod. We followed the rise and fall of the needle to the old galvanized pipes of the tub.

E-u-r-e-k-a! she'd said.

Looking back, I remember my heart aching even as we laughed so hard she cried. I'm not sure why. Did I think that this was coming to an end? I wanted to remember this sweet moment, to hold it in my mind, suspended.

Following Stella's new theory, we decided to start with Antietam because there would be almost no chance of missing whatever was left. My thinking went something like this; if we picked up absolutely nothing, then that would force Stella to think about just what she was asking for when she asked for LaLa. After all, I was the one there in the room with her. Me. What would it take for her to stop looking behind and finally see me in front of her?

At night, in Sharpsburg, my uncle had told me, it becomes very, very dark, even on starry nights in the middle of the summer, even near the summer equinox. The dark settles in like a cloud of silent black birds. I didn't actually believe, not in the same way as Stella. But what if?

Long after Stella had drifted off to sleep in the single numbers of the night, I turned the EMF meter back on. I rested it near her and watched the needle. I lay there, and sweated, and tried not to worry, tried not to loop through events like Stella falling through a black iron railing.

Why was it that, by instinct and a certain crawling feeling on the back of my neck, I made sure to never look in that particular corner by the stairs up to the widow's walk in the middle of the night? There was no reason to look.

Stella's breath was here, slow and heavy on my arm, part of the house's calm, old, night, punctuated by the wind seeping in through the slats in the walls. This was before the threatening and hostage-taking words appeared, the words written in scratchy felt-tip pen in small capital letters on the back of the EMF manual, left by accident outside on the patio, and the half-written word written in blood on the attic wall, but never finished.

Next on the list: recording devices. A visual recorder needed to be sensitive enough to record in the near-total black, or the blacker than night, of the Antietam battlefield. I bought one secondhand at a pawn shop in the old railroad town near us.

We tested the camera, and she posed for me, but always reluctantly. She didn't like being the center of attention, and there's something about a camcorder that changes things. This was when camcorders were still fairly large, fitting into the meat of a man's palm, a strap wrapping around the knuckles.

There was a lot of "noise" in the digital screen playback, but she always looked so fresh and beautiful, even with fuzzy edges and the color bleed from the RGB pixels. I prize those recordings from that green, hot, summer and keep copies, first on CD and now USBs, in a bank safety deposit box. Soon I'll have to make a decision about whether or not to transfer these to the cloud.

The Earnshays started leaving notes with an increasingly nasty edge. First it was about the rent, which was, of course, always late, and then non-existent. Then it was about the need to clean up a little better. Then it was about needing to move my bike because the tires were flattening against the ground. The last notes were about evictions and hiring an attorney, which they were loath to do.

I didn't care. We didn't care. We were together, and I usually walked down to the corner liquor store to pick up some cheap tuna, mayo, and white bread. She stayed behind, always. Nix had been seen driving around slowly, too slowly for anyone's good. Gross food for summer, but better than the round, plastic wheel of bologna, smeared blue ink dates well past expiration. Everything was so dreamy and warm and so weirdly calm that I don't think I even felt angry about Nix at that time. This was the warm round globe I lived in, at the top of the house, with Stella. Time slipped forward and backward. No one could enter it without our permission.

But then summer leaned closer in early August, the dog days. The sun slanted directly now into our windows, and the attic became unbearable. We gathered up enough change to buy beat-up box fans and put them in two dormer windows at opposite ends, one to pull in warm air and one to push out hot, stale air, now leavened with the smell of dust, dried-up bugs, and old cigars from a long-ago haunt of the widow's walk.

Most of that summer I wore only cut-off jeans and cheap blue shower flip-flops that began to curl up. There was something primal and animal about seeing my body become leaner and sinewy as the thermostat crept higher and higher. Stella's white tank top and the recordings, of course, were the wonder of my days.

I settled on August 1, 1996 as the day of the Antietam investigation. That year I ended up not going until September 17, but that, oddly enough, ended up being appropriate because that was the actual start day of the Battle of Antietam.

September 17 began with a chill, a bright, beautiful, sunny day, the kind of morning that normally would make you feel glad to be alive, made you feel like you survived the summer. I recognized that deceptive morning light when it came again, five years later, on 9/11.

The trick was to make it into the park before dark and hide when the rangers made their final sweep before locking down the Visitor Center for the night. My goal was to hide out in or behind Dunker Church and wait until midnight. I put on a long-sleeved dark shirt and my black church pants, loaded my gear in a small backpack.

The church, a low, one-story, brick building painted white, was not the original Dunker Church that the Dunkers worshipped in while cannons fired from the battlefields, the same sloping fields our Beuna Vista widow walk overlooked. It's a reconstruction, just like everything else. But when I slipped inside the cool quiet of the church, the dark floor and simple, dark wooden pews made me feel as though I'd entered a coffin. No, that's not the right word. I'd entered an empty mausoleum. Not a church and not a coffin, but something in between. White outside, dark and cool and still inside. The dark, small, animal pounding of my heart reminded me I needed to be quiet.

A ranger took a quick peek inside but didn't see me sitting in the back pew. I saw the latchkey drop. This was before the parks began to be visited regularly by paranormal teams and retired Civil War tourists and scavengers. I guess you could say I was one of the first.

I waited. Then I moved outside and watched the last of the sun fade and the moon rise.

Just as I'd been warned, the battlefields stretched out, darker than the dark, the only light coming from the white outlines of field statues, frozen forever in mid-action. It was eerie, but this was where I needed to be.

Slowly, I made my way to Miller's Cornfield, the site of some of the battle's worst carnage. If there were going to be any sightings from disturbed, uneasy, spirits, they would converge there. Or maybe Sunken Road, but that would have to wait for another time. I wasn't ready for Sunken Road.

I nearly tripped and fell over several of the War Department tablets, angled at just the right angle to stab me. Those dry recountings of who was where and which unit went which direction—where had these details come from? From soldiers' letters home or from the generals who dropped down into their camp chairs and wrote candle-lit dispatches back to Lincoln and Davis?

At least that much was known, even if it felt too dry and stiff and incomplete. No wonder the number of mediums and spiritualists exploded after the Civil War; everyone wanted to know. Maybe not to know the horrible and wrenching details of the last moments—who can bear that? But maybe to get some confirmation that the tie that binds is still there. That death is not the end.

There was—creepily enough—still corn in the cornfield. Row upon row upon row of corn past the peak, now beginning to turn brown. The cornstalks stood in dark rows, alert and attentive, and the hair on the back of my neck rose. I almost turned back.

Even now I'm not sure why I stayed, but what I do know is that I saw something. Maybe just the cornstalks rubbing against each other. If Stella had been with me, I would have brought her close to me.

I crouched low so I couldn't be seen—why, I'm not sure—was I afraid of a spirit seeing me? My hands shaking, I turned on my camcorder. I sat and waited for my eyes to adjust, but they never did. The dark only deepened, and there was a feeling of something gathering, rustling, congealing in that field.

Then—I swear—I saw something float out of the stalks—a round shape like someone hunched over and crawling on all fours. Just barely—almost a suggestion, an imprint against the dark. Then another, the size and shape of a child or a woman's back, rounded. No features, just a shape wearing itself.

My throat tightened and all I could feel was the roaring of my blood and the air pushing in and out of my chest in hot, tight, gasps. Everything narrowed to the edge of the cornfield and the shapes emerging, one by one, rolling forward then disappearing, rolling, then gone. I held on as long as I could, my camcorder shaking but still running. The red light pulsed.

Hold, hold, hold on. Her hand in mine.

I stood and waved at the round shapes rolling and emerging from the field. She would see me. A dark bird in my chest heaved and flew up and out.

In front of me, cornstalks shook and fell. A group of teenagers in summer shorts and t-shirts flew out, running, their bare arms and legs flashing, flashing, falling, hopping, then gone.

Their car lights flashed and spun over the fields as they careened over speed bumps. I laid myself down. The ground pressed up and into me, gravel pocking my face and long blades of grass tickling my neck and forehead.

This is how it felt. This is what I'd come to the field to know. It nearly killed me, but at least I knew. This was not her cornfield, but if she was anywhere, it would be here, at the pathway.

I poured my hot breath into the ground, dug the points of my knees into gravel, clawed her name into the dirt and broken cornstalks. Heart: blood and bone: water.

Years later, after Nix was found guilty and locked up based on the evidence he'd left behind in the widow's walk, I found the video those kids made. Someone from that group, now in their 30s, had posted it on YouTube. Someone else debunked it by pointing out they'd made those shapes by blowing big soap bubbles.

Every year on August 7th, I still go back to the cornfield where she was found, one week after she'd been killed and carried off.

Someday she'll answer back. It won't be a sound, but it will be something that I will see. I will know it for what it is.

UNDERSTANDING

KELSEY M. YOUNG

Of the several professors who complained of his comprehension difficulties, one recommended that Bryant come see me. With the depth of his difficulties, it was a miracle he made it into Bell University. We were known as the best university for the oral and speaking deaf who lived within Milan; not so much for those who weren't oral.

The shy young man opened my office door a crack, making my floor vibrate. "Hello? Are you Dr. Natasha? They said you could help me."

"Come in." I turned to face him and the door opened wider. Dark-haired and tall, Bryant had the gangly look that so many first-year students have, and he lacked the confidence of most. But his smile, though nervous, was genuine. "Sit down." I pointed to the seat across from mine.

He sat, shifting a little. Most of my students struggled with starting this conversation, but Bryant surprised me by getting right to the point. "My professors said I'm missing a lot of information in class. I don't get why. If I can see them talk, I can catch what they're saying. When I can't do that, they sound all mixed up."

"I see." I brought up his records on my screen. When I spoke, I turned to face him. "Your chart says you're high-functioning and don't need aids. Is that correct?"

"Yes. People don't believe me when I say I don't need aids! One audiologist told me I was this close to not qualifying for being deaf." He grinned as he held his index finger and thumb a milliunit apart, indicating he had only a mild hearing loss.

"Aids are not the problem," I said. His audiogram was close to perfect. "How do you do in class?"

"Okay. I read their lips."

I moved closer to him, to show I valued what he had to say. Many people with comprehension difficulties lacked respect from their peers and elders.

"If they turn around, I'm screwed," Bryant continued. "I did okay with some of my high school classes, because the teachers in those classes always faced us. But some insisted on writing on the holoboard while talking at the same time. I miss a lot in class."

"How did you succeed enough to enter Bell University?" The latter type of teacher he described was far more common here, given that nearly everyone in Milan—and certainly every "Lanner" employed at Bell University—took listening skills for granted. Children who couldn't adapt to Milan's ways were sent down lower paths early on.

Bryant sat up more and his smile widened more than usual for Lanners. "I'm bright. My mom says I started reading early, and I learned how to understand people through the garble. Basic survival skills." One of his shoulders tilted forward in a shrug, another oddity for a Lanner.

"Have you looked into other ways of getting information? Can you get notes from your friends?"

"I don't have a lot of friends here who I can copy notes from."

I had always thought it problematic that students here were forced to rely on each other for notes, in the classic group mentality of Milan. That was one problem with moving to a different country on Eyeth, this colony planet of deaf people: dealing with narrow-minded people in one's new country. My home country, Pegasus, had universities that were better for all, with professors providing a basic set of notes to expand on in class. But Pegasus allowed for multiple ways of communicating: speaking as well as various sign languages. Milan, compared to Pegasus, was pitiful with its reliance on speaking. "And that's blocking your success here? Less resources?"

Bryant nodded. "I think so."

On my screen, I called up a boilerplate form for the notetaker request, added his name and the date, and sent it to his student address. "Send this form to the professors you have difficulties with," I told him. "This will give them permission to call up a notetaker for you. Next week we'll discuss other ways of dealing with your situation."

Bryant's eyebrows creased upward in a wince. It was always humiliating, being forced to ask for help, but it was the first step of many. The line of his mouth tightened and he nodded. "I'll send it out. Thank you so much, Dr. Natasha."

"You're welcome. See you same time, next week."

After he left, I typed out the basic diagnostic paperwork for his records. Some of my previous students had managed to complete a degree with only my notetaker forms. That was great ... until the day they left university. Prevailing wisdom in Milan was that, past high school age, these struggling young people no longer needed assistance. They were expected to sink or swim upon entering university or the real world.

As the Comprehension Coordinator, my job was to provide assistance for those students with difficulties. A previous president had inaugurated my job title as a way to increase the graduation rate. It had worked so well, I was the third to hold the position. My predecessors, like me, earned little respect from faculty. Half of them hated me, even though my position was badly needed, because I could walk any of their students away from speaking and toward communicating like the so-called animals in other countries. If they had to be animals to be happy, so be it.

But it was worth it when you saw the huge smile on a previously-struggling student's face, reporting that his GPA went up or that he found a decent job after graduating. For most cases, I had found, it was a simple matter of adjusting their aids and showing them how to consult an audiologist out in the real world for periodic adjustments. The notetaker, for them, was a short-term need.

Then there were a few cases like Bryant. Many didn't have aids. Some got by with a long-term notetaker. So many struggled out in the real world. I'd had some of them contact me again later on, desperate. For the difficult cases, there was a drastic solution, one that involved leaving Milan.

The next week Bryant returned. "Hi," he said. "What will we do today?"

I said, "Let's have a discussion. What do you know about nonverbal language?"

He squirmed, a typical response. Lanners had been taught from infancy that verbal language was of the utmost importance and never to acknowledge nonverbal language. This would be difficult. Finally, he managed, "... um, expressions?"

"Expressions! Very good! What kind?"

"When you're happy, you ..." Bryant forced a rictus. "When you're sad, you ..." His lips bent into a cartoonish frown. "Is that what you mean?"

"Yes," I said. "Basic expressions. I don't think you realize this, but Lanners here in Milan have subtle expressions compared to other people on Eyeth. I'll show you what non-subtle expressions look like." I expanded my screen to fill a wall and set the program I brought up on interactive mode. "Take a look." The program showed a blank human face. To its right, there were six slider bars, each representing a specific universal expression: happiness, sadness, anger, fear, surprise, and disgust. "Come up here," I encouraged him.

Bryant walked up to the projection, hesitating. "What do I do?"

"Try it out. Move a slider."

The expression on the face changed from blank to a Lanner's happy expression: corners of the mouth turned up slightly, eyes barely crinkled. "Oh!"

"Move it back. Try the others."

He tried each one in turn, moving the sliders enough to see what he recognized. "Okay. Six expressions. So?"

"Emotions are complicated. Why don't you try two together, see what you get?"

Bryant tried "disgust" and "happiness" together. He struggled with this for a while. "Huh?"

"Did you ever make jokes about disgusting things when you were young?"

Bryant thought for a moment. "Yes! My friends and I once got in trouble because we were laughing too loudly at a squashed bug and we made faces like that, but bigger." He pointed to the cartoon face. "The teachers told us not to open our mouths so wide when we laughed. Then they had us sit with clothespins on our lips to be sure they wouldn't open so wide again."

"See? You've experienced showing non-subtle

expressions like this before. Why don't you try mixing some others? If one brings something to mind for you, tell me." I was impressed with how quickly he caught on.

"Okay." He moved around the slider bars. "You'd be surprised and angry at the same time if you saw a burglar in your house."

"Very good! Why don't you try moving the sliders all the way, see how extreme each expression can get?"

He made a lot of progress in that session. At the end, I told him, "Bryant, this session was the first in a course that I teach to a few of my students."

"What kind of course?" His eyes narrowed.

"It's designed to teach you how to better understand all aspects of communication in order to improve your comprehension. The first part deals with facial expressions, and the second deals with unconscious gestures. We'll discuss the third part if you decide to continue down that path."

"How will this help?"

"Suppose you saw someone who was angry and you couldn't understand what they were saying. Would you start a fight with them?"

"No."

"One of my students came to me with that problem. Many students who have comprehension difficulties haven't picked up on the finer points of body language. If you can read someone, then it's easier to get the gist of what they're saying."

"What else do I need to do for this course?"

"Nonverbal language is more important than you think. Homework for next week is to name five incidents where you show an emotion or someone tells you not to do something like making a face. Next week, same time."

A week later Bryant returned with eight incidents. "First, I wanted this new food for dinner, but I couldn't catch what the cafeteria lady said it was since she was wearing a facemask. I got frustrated because I couldn't point at it so I had to ask for something I knew instead. Second, I noticed that one of my friends always sits on his hands. I asked him why. He said everyone in his family gestured before Milan banned it generations ago, so now it's a weird family quirk. Third, I shrugged my shoulders instead of raising my eyebrows and a teacher called me out for it. Fourth ..."

I smiled internally as he described the other incidents. I'd had some stoic students who struggled with showing their emotions and could take weeks before we could work through the first part of the course. "Good job, Bryant!" I told him. "We'll keep working on nonverbal concepts. Let's talk about gestures ... Yes?"

Bryant had stood to indicate he had a question, as was typical in the Lanner classroom, since teachers forbade students from raising their hands. Then he sat down. "Um, what does nonverbal language have to do with comprehension?"

"You can pick up on more body language cues from people. Subtlety is everything in comprehension." I didn't need him reporting me to faculty. Lanner teachers from preschool on forbade all forms of gesture. If a teacher needed to point out something, they would verbally describe it. I'd had students tell me stories of grade school teachers hitting their hands with a ruler if they went beyond the boundaries of their desk.

At this point, anything he learned about nonverbal language would be beneficial. Some of my students had been willing to learn comprehension of facial expressions but refused to learn gestures. Years later these students thanked me for helping them learn how to cope better in Milan.

He accepted this. We discussed natural gestures that still occurred to a small degree in Lanner society. I asked Bryant to expand on those. Young children who didn't have experience with descriptions were the only ones allowed to point. Bryant described the subtler pointing practices he knew of, like his buddy saying he saw a hot girl at three o'clock.

I decided to address a problem often seen in my students. "How do you get people's attention?"

Bryant chewed on his lip. "When I was a kid, I used to wave a lot. I got in trouble for that up to the end of elementary school, so I stopped. I still forget that I have to yell instead of wave sometimes."

"That's all right." Gestures came so naturally to Bryant that I was confident he would go through with the full course. But there was no need to mention that to him yet.

We then discussed body language, like how people tensed when they got nervous. Eventually I said, "Next week, same time?"

"Sure." He gave me a tentative smile. "I can't wait to see you again. This helped a lot."

"That's great to hear."

The next week, however, he never came. Concerned, I sent a reminder.

He got back to me a week later: "I think I got enough."

I sent another reminder.

It took him three weeks to respond: "Thanks. My notetaker helps now."

I was patient, having seen this in other students. Some completed the first two parts of the course and felt they could get by. Within six months to a year, those students would return, frustrated because they weren't.

So I waited. I took on other students who needed help with comprehension and attended staff meetings. A month later, I met with other comprehension professionals across Milan in a virtual conference to help them design a listening comprehension test for elementary-school aged children. A teacher from Braidwood thought if the comprehension problem was caught and corrected early enough, they wouldn't struggle later. I argued for those who may not benefit from early intervention. "What if oral methods don't work at all?"

"Then what? Foster them out to a manual family?" was the response from the Braidwood teacher. His virtual face raised an eyebrow a few milliunits, as if to say, *"Who do you think you're kidding, interloper?"*

I gritted my teeth and remembered why I had left a great country like Pegasus, which used multiple modes of communication. The people in one-method countries, like Milan, were so inflexible that they didn't understand. And I didn't have time for their nonsense. I said yes, that was one possibility, but we also had to design options that worked for the student's family. That didn't involve resorting to separation.

I didn't see Bryant again until a full year later when he burst into my office in tears. He sat down, unable to speak for a few minutes. Then he cleared his throat, wiped his cheeks, and said, "One of my professors refuses to let me use a notetaker."

That was a difficult situation I'd seen with many of my students. It drove most to complete the course with me. "I see. Do you need more help?"

Bryant looked at me, his eyes red. "What else is there?" He rubbed at his eyes, one at a time.

"There are non-oral methods you could look into." Making the leap was always difficult, but it was something that had to be done slowly.

"How will that help with oral comprehension? Manual isn't allowed in Milan." Now he was starting to understand.

I started with diagnostic questions. "Do you have to look at people to understand them?"

"Yes."

"Can you use the Telfono system?"

"Not with voice only."

"Can you understand what a person says if their back is turned to you?"

"Not really."

"All right." I turned to my screen and typed out my hunch to one of my co-workers. "I want to have someone else in my department diagnose you before we go further."

"Why?"

"I want to make sure you don't have anything else blocking your abilities. Go see Dr. Truzone, who's a few doors down from me. He'll give you a few tests."

Bryant hesitated, leaning back in his chair.

I smiled warmly. "I promise you, since he's in my department, he won't bite your head off if you don't understand him right away. He's seen many students struggle like you, and he's also seen many of them give up. Believe me, Dr. Truzone would hate seeing a promising young man like you not be able to succeed, and so would I. Can you go see him tomorrow?"

Bryant nodded once.

"Great. Come see me next week, same time!"

A few days later Dr. Truzone came in, making the floor vibrate. I looked up from my holoscreen, and he held out a small thick metal disk. "I think you're right."

I took the disk and tapped the center to bring up a holoprojection of the results. As I suspected, Bryant had auditory verbal agnosia, also seen in previous students. All of these students struggled with comprehending others' speech, so they were assumed to be profoundly deaf, even if their audiograms said otherwise. "Thank you." I put it down on my desk. "What do you think?"

Truzone laced his fingers together. "I talked to him. He's been adapting for years. He had an accident when he was young, creating the lesion that caused his agnosia. He said he could understand more when he was little, but he didn't know why his parents and teachers yelled at him more and more about not understanding as he got older, since his hearing hadn't changed."

I nodded. "And it's progressive, his agnosia?"

"Yes. No reversal possible right now. Most Lanner doctors aren't interested in agnosia, or even believe that it's an actual condition. They think the patients with agnosia aren't trying hard enough to understand." He twisted his mouth at this and shook his head. "I heard of a surgeon who wants to do research with stem cells to fix the lesions that cause it."

"It'd need widespread support before surgery is possible. Good to know for future students."

Truzone raised his eyebrows for his *gimme-something* look. "Any other new cases for me?"

"No." I paused to think. "Bryant is interesting. He saw me for a few weeks last year before giving up."

Truzone's eyes crinkled. "I think he'll stick around."

"Yes, he will. But he needs to follow through."

Bryant came back for his next appointment and sat down in the chair, getting to the point. "What's my diagnosis?"

"You have auditory verbal agnosia."

The space between his eyebrows creased. "What does that mean?"

"Your brain has difficulties with processing what other

people say. In plain English? It's hard for you to understand words."

"So I wasn't an idiot because I didn't try hard enough to understand? It wasn't me, it was my brain?" Bryant sat there, processing this, his face blank. "What does that mean for me?"

"There's an experimental procedure opening up in a few years. This surgeon wants to use stem cells to repair lesions in the brain, including the ones that cause agnosia. You'd be out of university by the time he's ready to start trials."

Bryant scowled, his mouth turning down more than a Lanner's would. He was young and impatient, but he was making progress with nonverbal language. "What else?"

"You did very well with recognizing expressions and using gestures ... That's only the surface. You have the option to go further, learn manual methods of communication, and then transfer to a university where you will do better."

His face twisted. Lanners weren't subtle when it came to the dislike of their former signing masters. "I don't know. Do I have to learn another language?"

"No, you don't," I told him, leaning forward. "You can learn manual English. Some of my students chose to learn Ameslan, but it's up to you." American Sign Language, shortened to Ameslan, was the language of the animals in Clerc. The rare few Lanners in this country with family or friends who already knew the language were usually the only ones willing to learn it.

Bryant leaned back. "I don't know."

"I know you like Milan." How could he not? He didn't know any better. "I have to warn you: your adult life here will be difficult. It will be like living on Old Earth. Milan is not happy about citizens who struggle with their way of life, so you will have little support. Think about the notetaker you have—that is the only support you will receive in your entire adult life. Unless you get lucky enough to find someone else who's patient enough to write back and forth with you or will face you while talking clearly. For a better life, you must learn a better way of communicating so that you can go to a country that will accommodate you."

He thought on this for a long time, his chin resting in his hands. Then like most of my students, Bryant chose the safer option: "I want to learn manual English."

"Very good." I brought up a form on the screen and handed him a silver stylus. "Read this carefully before you sign." It was a nondisclosure agreement, saying that he wouldn't tell another faculty member what I was doing unless they were in my department. It also warned him of the various dangers he could encounter through taking the remainder of this course: bullying, expulsion, deportation, and so on. I created this form after my first three years of working here and encountered much less trouble afterward.

Bryant read it, his eyes widening at the consequences, but signed anyway. "Where do we begin?"

We started with the alphabet. I gave him the homework of memorizing the alphabet and sent him a form with the handshapes on it.

His fingerspelling was satisfactory at the next session, so we moved through various levels of manual English over the next several weeks. His hands were slow at first, but I could tell he would be a good signer. Pity he had shackled himself to manual English.

As we progressed, he spoke less and signed more. There were a few times where he signed and spoke at the same time, but I always reprimanded him for that. "Don't mix your methods," I warned him. "Some people look down on those who use any form of oral. I don't want you making enemies."

He got it. From then on, he only spoke when he absolutely had to. Bryant seemed very enamored by manual English. Once he signed to me, *"I love those times—it's when my hands can be free."* I'd seen him around campus fingerspelling to himself, so I knew his time here was limited.

Near the end of the first half of that year, my department head came to see me. "I'd like to talk to you about Bryant Thomas."

"What is it?"

"I've received several complaints from his professors about 'twitchy hands' in class. Is he almost finished with the full manual course?"

"Yes. We haven't discussed transitioning yet, however."

He grimaced. "Make it fast. They're talking about throwing him out if he keeps this up. You want him ready when that happens."

At our next appointment, I told Bryant, "We need to talk about where you will go after you're out of this university in a few weeks."

"Out? I thought I had until the end of the year."

"I've received some complaints that you've been signing in class." I switched to signing. *"Practicing outside of your dormitory?"*

He slumped over. "Sorry," he mumbled. Then he sat up. *"I can't help it. It fits so well."*

"I know. That's why we need to talk about your transition. You need to emigrate."

"Where would I go?"

"To a country that signs English, meaning you have the option of either Fence or Pegasus. Fence is all manual English, but Pegasus is a melting pot of communication methods. They have a large community for manual English there." I spoke since it was complicated and I needed him to understand.

"Fence. I want to be around all people who sign English like me."

That was a common enough option for those from a one-method country who were too terrified of the concept of a multi-method country. "All right. Next week we're making a field trip to the capital for your emigration papers."

"How long will that take?"

"We can expedite the process by informing them of your diagnosis. Normally it can take months, but with a diagnosis, it's a few weeks. That will be enough time for you to finish out your classes."

We went to the capital, Clarke, the next week, a short trip away via a maglev train. I escorted him to the Emigration Building and informed the official of his AVA diagnosis, providing a copy of the paperwork signed by Dr. Truzone. She sent us to the window on the end, where Bryant received a tablet with the forms he had to fill out.

After entering all the information with the attached stylus, he returned it and the woman told him, "You will receive your card and train ticket in a few weeks. Be prepared to depart." As part of the emigration policies for their "failures," the Milan government paid for their departure tickets.

Bryant returned to the university with me. In my office, he signed, "*What will I do when I get there?*"

"I have contacts in Fence. One of my former students there can provide you with a room until you go away to university. Did you look up universities like I asked you to?"

"I applied to some as a transfer student."

"*Very good.* Next week we'll discuss transferring with the dean here."

Bryant gulped, his face pale.

"Don't worry. He won't swallow you whole." I gave him a reassuring smile.

He smiled back shakily.

We met again a week later and talked to the dean. He seemed happy to get Bryant out of his school and told him, "Personally, I think professors should respect their students' needs more, but I didn't design this country's mindset. I'm sorry you had a difficult time with us, young man."

Bryant blinked, taken aback. "Oh, uh, thank you."

"So you're transferring to Port Arthur?"

"Yes. They offered me a scholarship."

"Good people there. We've had previous students transfer there as well. I wish you the best of luck."

They shook hands, and the dean finalized Bryant's paperwork on his screen. I had already contacted Michal, who Bryant would be staying with in Fence. Michal confirmed that he would be there at the train station in Fence to pick him up.

At our final meeting, I asked Bryant, *"What about your parents? Aren't they concerned that you're leaving?"*

"My mom knows I struggle with understanding. My dad isn't too happy. He thinks I need to learn how to adapt better, but he doesn't get it."

"I'm sorry."

"Don't worry about it. I promised my mom I'd write her letters. Will you see me off?"

"Certainly." I smiled. *"When do you depart?"*

"December thirtieth, from the station in Glenmoor at noon."

We hugged, then he departed my office for the last time.

From what I heard, he did well on his finals, despite his professors' efforts. The only one he struggled with was the one with the professor who refused to give him a notetaker, but he scraped by with a middling grade.

On December thirtieth, I took a car to the station at Glenmoor. I walked up the steps to the platform shortly before noon and saw that many people were there. No doubt all were emigrants. Some were families, with crying children, and some were young adults like Bryant, who I saw standing with his trunk full of his worldly possessions. I went over to him and signed, "*Hello!*"

He flinched. "Shouldn't you speak here?"

"No, it's fine. You need to learn how to sign out in the open," I told him. "*Your world will soon expand from my office to a whole country! You need to adjust.*"

Bryant had to smile at that. "*Yeah, I will. I talked to Michal a bit through this Fence messaging program—they call it Rapier over there, not Telfono. He seems great.*"

"*He is. I taught him the same things I taught you, and he's done very well. You'll do great there, Bryant.*"

"*Thanks, Dr. Natasha. I think I will.*"

"*Don't think. Do!*"

The sleek maglev train, bright red against the bleak gray December sky, pulled up. Bryant looked from the train to me. "Here I go."

I watched him show the ticket to the conductor and wave to me from the window before the train took off.

He would do very well in the years to come. I heard about him through Michal for a while, then nothing after graduating. Many years later he wrote me a letter. "I can't imagine my life anywhere else but here," he told me. "I love my wife, our children, what I'm doing right now. If I was still in Milan, I'd be miserable. Thank you."

ONLINE DATING
DANIEL CROSBY

In the center of the table, there was a large bouquet that obscured our view of each other. We both reached for it, but Leonardo got there first. I let him move the mass of silk flowers to the side. When I saw his face again, I remembered how much I had lucked out—he was even hotter in person than in his profile. A few years younger than me, but that was okay.

I smiled at him. <Thank you, Leo> I signed.

He smiled back. <You're welcome, Jay.>

<What did you think of the show?>

Still smiling, Leo stared off into the distance. Figuring he was gathering his thoughts, I waited a few moments for Leo to say something. But he didn't.

<Leo?>

<Yes?> he said, puzzled. <Did you understand me?>

<What? No?>

<But you have the glasses> he said.

Indeed I did. Everyone did, even hearing people. Whenever someone else said something, your glasses captured every aspect of that event: the words themselves, the person's pupil dilation, their respiration, their perspiration, their body temperature, and other minutiae. The glasses then crunched all that data and scrolled real-time analysis of the conversation across the bottom of your vision.

But I didn't care about all that just now.

<Yes, I do> I replied. <What does that have to do with anything?>

<Don't you have a Chip?> Leo tapped his right frontal lobe and, for the first time, I noticed a centimeter-length scar just underneath his hairline.

I grimaced. <No, I don't.>

<Oh> he said. <Why not?>

<I just ... don't.> Call me old-fashioned, but the truth is that I just didn't trust the things. I liked Clear Channel's glasses, but the introduction of their Chips had added a wrinkle. The surgical implant allowed the user to react to the stream of data emanating from their conversational partner by mentally visualizing a pre-defined icon. It was a laughably narrow range—you could only express emotions such as "like," "love," and "laughing." Your reactions were then uploaded publicly to Clearnet so that anyone, including, say, your date could see them. Well, anyone with a Chip, anyway.

Neither of us said anything for a while.

<Well> he said <I 'liked' the show.> The way Leo signed 'like' made it clear that he meant that he had 'liked' the post on Clearnet.

<That's great> I said. Unable to stop myself, I snarked, <Why didn't you just display a thumbs-up in meatspace?>

Leo blinked, confused. Then it dawned on him. <Oh! Like, the 'like' symbol?>

I sighed. Now I felt old. <Yes. Nevermind. Let's order our food.>

<Sure> Leo said.

We both looked down at the tablecloth. The composite plastic and silicon material displayed shimmering images of tasty-looking food next to numbers. I tapped on my usual order—number 76—and it blinked to let me know that the kitchen had received my order.

When I looked up, Leo was still looking at the menu. He spent a considerable amount of time pausing at each image before moving on to the next.

I lightly tapped the table to get his attention. When he looked up, I said <I've eaten here before. Any questions?>

Leo pushed his glasses up the bridge of his nose. <Maybe. What did you order?>

<Number 76> I said. <It's delicious.>

Leo looked at that image. <But it only has four stars on Clearnet. Some of the reviews are just two stars.>

I buried my face in my hands. This was going to be a *long* night.

TOMMY GOES TO COLLEGE
CHRISTOPHER JON HEUER

Like all the kids, Tommy too begged his parents for a double amputation so he could print his own legs.

"All the guys have amputations now!" he said, sliding the flashcast of the most recent *Sports Illustrated* across the table toward Dad. "Look at these prosthetics! You can get the same designs the NFL has!"

"Yeah, if I sell the house!" Dad said. He wanted nothing more in the world than to help his son get his legs amputated, hell, even both arms! But the surgery alone—per limb!—was a small fortune, and it was either an amputation or a car. And that didn't even begin to cover all these newfangled specialized designs the kids were ordering. Sure, once you slipped them on you might fly with the fastest halfbacks in football history. But what good was an NFL contract if 20 years into your career you were still paying off the design you purchased to win Homecoming?

"But we've already got the printer, Dad!"

"And we're very happy to print your pads and cleats and everything else!"

"None of that stuff is going to help me though!"

Grandfather spoke up from his wheelchair at the end of the table. He was Old School, and saw this whole thing as ghastly. "Football's in here," he said, tapping his arthritic sternum with a gnarled knuckle. "And up here." The knuckle raised almost enough to tap his forehead but he couldn't get it up quite that high anymore.

"Grandfather, please." Tommy turned to Dad. "What if I sell my car? We can get just the right one amputated. There'd even be enough left over for one of those Joe Fricke designs!" Joe Fricke was the current quarterback of the UW-Madison Badgers. His time for a 40-yard dash held steady at 3.83 seconds, and once he got up to speed, he could easily average 34 miles per hour. Of course, Joe Fricke probably hadn't designed his legs but he sure did make a pretty penny off UW-Madison's use of his name for the marketing. And once you had an NFL contract, your name could be up there too! On even better designs!

"How are you going to get to work?" Dad asked.

"I'll run!"

Dad sighed, counted silently to five. "Okay. How are you going to pick up Becky for dates?"

That was a tougher question. Becky was one of the primary reasons Tommy enjoyed his car so much.

"I'm never going to get to college," he moaned.

Grandfather shook his head at the end of the table. "Ghastly. Ghastly," he muttered.

Dad rested his hand on his son's neck, patting it. "Just do your best." He decided to make a poor joke. "Look. You could always get tackled. Break your legs that way." He thought better of that statement though, when Tommy perked up. "And don't crash your car either!" Dad added.

Hustisford High School. Home of the Hustisford Falcons. The pep rally for the game against Juneau sucked majorly, and not just because the cheerleaders would have nothing to do with him. They would only carry around the Captains anyway. It was tradition to break your old legs at the rally during final period. It was against the rules to replace anything during the game, so everyone waited until the last second to print their new ones. You wanted the best equipment going onto the field ... hot off the presses, so to speak.

It was a show of team spirit for the other students to break the team's old stuff. The cheerleaders usually led the assault. Plenty of them had prosthetic legs too. There was no other way they could carry Tank McCannen; even on stumps he outweighed half of them combined.

Drumrolls thundered and the smashing began. Tommy watched, outwardly smiling and clapping along with the others, but inwardly he felt nothing but shame. Thank God for jeans. Anything to cover his muscles.

One boy had held back from the carnage. He was standing on the very top row of bleachers. Tommy saw him but didn't recognize him, though he did note just the barest hint of a purple t-shirt. An odd color, to be sure, especially in a gymnasium decked out in red and white. In fact the longer he looked the surer Tommy became that he had never seen the kid before. Nobody else was looking at him either, not until the boy took a blast horn out of his pocket and pressed the stud. It emitted a shriek that drowned out even the drums. People grabbed their ears, flinching. Then everyone turned to look.

The boy opened his jacket—too late Tommy remembered purple and white were Juneau's school colors—and pulled a nanopulse bomb from an inside pocket. Electromagnetic. One of the smart models. They gave off no physical blast, but the pulse was designed to take out phones and car batteries as well as power grids and the internal circuity of prosthetic limbs. Tommy recognized the design from *Sports Illustrated.* People were always trying to sneak them past stadium security. They were a real headache for the Packers. Bears fans were bitter.

"Juneau ... Trojans ... RULE!" the boy screamed into the shocked silence as he heaved the bomb into the air.

The overhead lights immediately flared and died, plunging the gymnasium into darkness. Startled shrieks filled the air, followed by clattering sounds as the cheerleaders toppled over, their prosthetics no longer stabilized now that the pulse had disrupted their built-in equilibrium sensors. The ones holding Tank hit especially hard. Tommy could have sworn he heard several bones break. Some people had all the luck.

Now people were screaming in earnest. A couple of lighters flickered on throughout the crowd. Those who could walk and grasp things moved to the doors and opened them. Pale sunlight spilled in from the hallway windows beyond.

Bedlam. Half the gym was crawling for the exits. Poor Brian Grady, the quarterback, was dragging himself along on one arm; that being the only limb he had left. Even Coach was on his ass, a place Coach would probably rather die than admit he was capable of visiting.

"EVERYBODY OUT OF THE GYM!" someone roared. "ASSEMBLE ON THE FRONT LAWN!"

But nothing could be done. The boy who had triggered the nanopulse bomb was long gone. Power throughout the whole town was out. It didn't matter if a building was still hooked up to the grid or if it had those new Smartglass windows. Everything was dead. Flashcasters. Tablets.

The school's 3-D sports equipment printer.

A hasty team meeting was assembled then and there.

"Someone must have a phone!" Tank yelled. He propped himself up against a tree and nearly lost his balance when it turned out nobody had one that worked. After that he didn't slam his fist on the ground anymore.

"All right," Brian said. "That bomb was a P-40. You can get them on eBay. Ten-mile range. Someone's gotta live outside of ten miles from here."

They all looked at Tommy.

"We have one printer!" Tommy snapped, more than a bit defensively. "And it's half-empty. We'll get like one leg!"

Coach spat on the grass. He was laying on his side so the gob didn't fly very far. "Anybody else?"

Several players did, along with a couple of the students within earshot. But ten miles was still ten miles, with no car to make the first leg of the trip. And only two hours until game time.

"Damn," said Coach. "We can't forfeit."

Nobody asked why. They knew. Equipment malfunction was not a legitimate excuse for forfeiture if enough players were mobile. And they had enough. Tommy. Half the second string. Almost all of the third. Players who hadn't deemed themselves good enough to even bother with amputations.

"Shit," Tank sobbed.

The Juneau Trojans rolled in an hour later, their bus the only moving vehicle anyone saw for a while. But slowly more of the townspeople began to trickle in, and then a bunch of other cars started to arrive. There would still be some sun for an hour or so, but some genius with a few replacement parts nonetheless got the field lights working by hooking them up to the functional cars. Someone asked if car batteries could run the school printer. Every Trojan supporter there was sure this wouldn't work.

Tommy led the warm-up. Coached bumped him up from halfback to quarterback. Brian promised to send him play signals but because he was seated Tommy could barely see him and soon stopped looking. Dad and Grandfather showed up. Grandfather's wheelchair was parked right at the end of the bleachers where the benched players sat, gripping tightly at the seats so they wouldn't topple over.

"Ghastly," Grandfather muttered over and over. He made sure Tommy heard this, too.

The first half was awful. All the Trojans' stuff worked fine. The second string Hustisford Falcon linemen, on the other hand, went flying in all directions. But Tommy didn't have to build up as much momentum to dodge the Trojans as they did to get at him, so after a while they started barreling right past, and Tommy started completing passes.

During halftime the Hustisford Math Club constructed their own nanopulse bomb, and detonated it at the fifty yard line during the start of the third quarter (with Hustisford trailing 63-6). This was a makeshift job, cobbled together from the shielded stuff in the Science lab. The range didn't extend much further than the field and parking lot, but it did the trick. With no car batteries left to run the field lights both teams were forced to forfeit, falling slightly yet equally in the overall sectional rankings.

Tommy still made out. His stats went up considerably, and his dodging impressed one of the recruiters. That summer he had a state-of-the-art double amputation, paid for by the UW-Madison Badgers. Upon recovery he played football, reprinted his legs time and time again, just as he always dreamed of doing, and made a lot of money.

Eventually even Grandfather approved.

BIOS

KRIS ASHTON is an Australian author best known for his tales of horror and dark speculative fiction. He has published three novels, more than thirty short stories, and is also a respected journalist. He lives in the wilds of southwestern Sydney with his wife, two children, and a slightly mad boxer dog.

JOHN LEE CLARK is the author, most recently, of *Where I Stand* (Handtype Press, 2014). His essays and poems have appeared in diverse publications, including *The Chronicle of Higher Education, McSweeney's, Poetry, The Seneca Review, Sign Language Studies*, and the *Minneapolis Star Tribune*. He lives in Hopkins, Minnesota, with the artist and author Adrean Clark, and their three sons. [johnleeclark.com]

MICHAEL R. COLLINGS—educator, literary scholar and critic, poet, novelist, essayist, columnist, reviewer, and editor—has explored science fiction, fantasy, and horror for three decades. He has been nominated three times for the Bram Stoker Award® (Horror Writers Association) for nonfiction and for poetry and was recently named a World Horror Convention Grand Master. Retired from Pepperdine University, he lives in Idaho.

WILLY CONLEY of Hanover, Maryland, is a professor of Theatre and Dance at Gallaudet University. He is an award-winning, internationally produced playwright whose writings have appeared in numerous anthologies and periodicals. He has a novel, *The Deaf Heart*, and a book of plays, *Vignettes of the Deaf Character and Other Plays*.

BOBBY COX is from lush Washington State and now lives in San Francisco with Joanne Yee. He read voraciously as a child and has been writing since high school. He works as a developer at the University of California, Berkeley. "Rui's Story" is Bobby and Joanne's first collaboration: Bobby wrote while Joanne created. Language deprivation is real and has a devastating impact on Deaf children worldwide.

DANIEL CROSBY was born deaf in 1988, and he has been a sci-fi fan for about as long. He grew up mainstreamed. In the late '90s, several events happened almost simultaneously: he learned ASL at deaf camp, he got a cochlear implant, and he discovered the Internet. Today Daniel spends most of his free time reading sci-fi, tinkering with computers, and riding his bicycle. He lives in Los Angeles, California.

MARSHA GRAHAM is a retired attorney who co-authored a workbook on passing the essay portion of the bar. She's written for newspapers, created technical manuals, and been published in a legal magazine. She blogs, guest blogs, is a public speaker, and edits for a fiction author. Her first blog was on the trials and tribulations of hearing loss. She's been published in other venues, including the *Bridges Anthology* of the East Texas Writers Guild.

KRISTEN HARMON has published fiction, creative nonfiction, and academic essays in literary magazines, peer-reviewed scholarly journals, literary anthologies, and edited chapter collections. She is a professor of English at Gallaudet University. She and her colleague, Jennifer Nelson, have co-edited two collections of prose writing by Deaf Americans with Gallaudet University Press (1830-1930 and 1980-2010). She is the series editor of Gallaudet University Press's Classics in Deaf Studies and has edited and written the introduction for volumes in the series.

CHRISTOPHER JON HEUER is the author of *Bug: Deaf Identity and Internal Revolution* and *All Your Parts Intact: Poems*. His short stories and poetry have appeared in many anthologies and periodicals. He is a professor of English at Gallaudet University in Washington, D.C.

LILAH KATCHER's work has appeared in *Under a Shared Umbrella: Tales of Synchronicity and Happenstance, The Buff and Blue,* and *The Gallaudet Link*. In June 2014, she did a poetry residency at The Anderson Center in Red Wing, Minnesota (Deaf Artists Residency, funded by the National Endowment for the Arts). Lilah is an MFA student at American University where she is also the Nonfiction Editor for *FOLIO*.

DAVID LANGFORD has been publishing and writing about SF since 1975. Novels include *The Space Eater* and *The Leaky Establishment*; there are many collections of magazine reviews and criticism. Langford's 29 Hugo awards span several categories: Fanzine and Semiprozine for the newsletter *Ansible* (1979-current), Short Story for "Different Kinds of Darkness" (2000) and Related Work for the online *Encyclopedia of Science Fiction* (with John Clute and others). He has always had hearing problems. [ansible.uk]

RAYMOND LUCZAK is the author and editor of 19 books. His most recent titles include *The Kinda Fella I Am: Stories* and *The Kiss of Walt Whitman Still on My Lips*. His Deaf gay novel *Men with Their Hands* won first place in the Project: QueerLit Contest 2006. His work has been nominated seven times for a Pushcart Prize. A playwright, he lives in Minneapolis, Minnesota. [raymondluczak.com]

A. M. MATTE, an award-winning writer, was first published at the age of 11, and was a produced playwright by the age of 12. Recent publications include short stories in literary magazines *Virages* and *Ancrages* and collections *Where Pigeons Roost* and *Ce que l'on divulgue*. A. M. Matte's writing is supported by the Ontario Arts Council, the Toronto Arts Council, and the Canada Council for the Arts. [ammatte.ca]

BRIGHID MEREDITH enjoys a grim story. She loves watching characters evolve into villains, and she believes that the only difference between a hero and a scrub are circumstances—circumstances that can be tweaked until the would-be hero becomes an axe-murdering psychopath. After reading her work, some readers may be surprised to learn that Brighid is happily married to the woman of her dreams, and that she has four wonderful children whom she loves dearly. It's just that her passion is dark.

KRISTEN RINGMAN is a deaf writer, wanderer, and mother. She writes multi-cultural lyrical fiction and poetry inspired by her persistent wanderings to far-off places. She is the author of *I Stole You: Stories from the Fae* (Handtype Press) and *Makara: a novel* (Handtype Press), a Lambda Literary finalist in Debut Fiction, and the editor of *Everyday Haiku: an anthology* (Wandering Muse Press). She received her MFA from Goddard College. [kristenringman.com]

MAVERICK SMITH is a D/deaf, queer, Trans, disabled, non-binary settler-Canadian who tackles themes of equity and social justice in their writing. Maverick is honored to be included in this anthology. Previously, their poetry and prose has been published in *QDA: A Queer Disability Anthology* and *Brave Boy World: A Trans Man Anthology*. In 2016, Maverick was a featured author at Naked Heart: An LGBTQ Festival of Words which was presented by Glad Day Bookshop.

TONYA MARIE STREMLAU always wanted to be a writer, teacher, and mother, and she somehow ended up as all three. She lives in the metro Washington, D.C. area where she is raising twins, teaching English at Gallaudet University, and writing. Tonya became deaf from spinal meningitis during elementary school. She enjoys indoor rock climbing and cooking, particularly Cajun/Creole dishes to keep her from missing her hometown of New Orleans too much.

JACOB WARING aspires to be a journalist, creative writer and is an avid reader. He was the Editor-in-Chief of *The Voice*, Norwalk Community College's student newspaper. "The Tale of Two Prodigies" is the first of his short stories to be published. He is currently pursuing a bachelor's degree in journalism. He one day hopes to inspire change in the world through his written works and journalistic endeavors.

JOANNE YEE is a native San Franciscan from the heart of the Mission. She experienced growing up in a mixed SEE/Oral/PSE mainstreamed environment. Later, she grew to express herself through ASL learned from the Deaf community. She now works in the same elementary school that she attended as a student. She is passionate about Deaf children; helping them grow with visual play and expression.

KELSEY M. YOUNG, a semi-native of Colorado, graduated from Gallaudet University in 2013 with a BA in English. She grew up mainstreamed and is now bilingual in both English and ASL. Kelsey currently lives in the greater Denver area and is working on getting more of her writing out there.